Elspeth Cameron lives in the Highlands of Scotland, in the district of Lochaber. She is the author of three books: *In the Shadow of the Kelpie* (Pentland Press) and *In the Shadow of the Gun* and *Kirsten* (both Blackwater Press). She is a graduate of the Open University, her main line of study being history.

For my grandchildren

Y2Kids

Elspeth Cameron

WOLFHOUND PRESS
Celebrating 25 Years

First published in 1999 by
Wolfhound Press Ltd
68 Mountjoy Square
Dublin 1, Ireland
Tel: (353-1) 874 0354
Fax: (353-1) 872 0207

The Arts Council
An Chomhairle Ealaíon
Wolfhound Press receives financial assistance from The Arts Council/An Chomhairle Ealaíon, Dublin, Ireland.

British Library Cataloguing in Publication Data
A catalogue record for this book is available from the British Library.

ISBN 0-86327-761-6

10 9 8 7 6 5 4 3 2 1

Cover Illustration: Kevin McSherry
Cover Design: Reprolink
Typesetting: Wolfhound Press
Printed in the UK by Cox & Wyman Ltd, Reading, Berks.

ONE

'Claire?' Doyle glanced across the table. 'Any suggestions?'

She was the brains of their group. And what they needed was an idea — something to start from.

Claire tweaked at the legs of her spectacles. There were red marks at the tops of her ears. You'd think her parents would get her a new pair, thought Doyle.

'Something from history, maybe,' she suggested.

'*History*!' Brendan snorted, from where he sat next to her. 'We're talking a project on the millennium — on the year 2000! That's the future, not the past. We should be thinking space and the Internet and all that stuff. Not *history*.' He wrinkled his freckled nose in disgust.

Doyle looked nervously from one to the other. Miss Binchly had appointed him group leader — a sort of chairperson, she had said — and she had emphasised the need to involve all five people in the group; the project had to be a combined effort. She was busy at the far end of the classroom, marking papers, but Doyle knew she was keeping an eye on all six groups in the room.

'Why can't it be about the past *and* the future?' Desmond asked quietly.

'Back to the future,' Aisling giggled, from the other side of the table. 'Pity we haven't a time machine.'

'We probably don't need that,' Desmond said, with a glance in Claire's direction. 'Claire can take us back.'

'How?' Aisling demanded, staring at him.

Doyle joined in the laughter, and then wished he hadn't. Aisling's cheeks flamed bright red as she realised that she'd been slow to get what Desmond meant. She never seemed to understand things unless they were put dead plainly.

Desmond hadn't laughed. 'She's good at history,' he explained simply.

'But what's the point?' Brendan demanded peevishly. 'We should concentrate on computers and all that.'

'That's the point,' Doyle interrupted. 'Everyone will be doing just that. We want something different.' He glanced at Claire. 'Had you thought of anything particular?' he asked.

'Just that we might be able to find something that happened at the beginning of this millennium and tune into that. There could be a link somewhere.' She looked at Brendan. 'Maybe we can bring in computers and the Internet somehow.'

'Maybe,' Brendan admitted grudgingly. 'What do you think, Doyle?'

'It's a start, anyway,' Doyle said. 'Desmond? Aisling? Will we try it?'

Aisling nodded. She won't want to say anything more just now, Doyle thought; she'll be afraid we might laugh at her again.

It wasn't that Aisling was stupid, or anything like that; she got good marks for most of her written work. It was just that her mind didn't seem to register things as quickly as everyone else's. She needed more time to think things through. Doyle's heart had sunk when Miss Binchly included her in his group — probably to balance the fact that they had Claire. Maybe he could get her to do most of the writing-up ....

Desmond was more forthcoming. 'It'll take a bit of research,' he said. 'We'll have to find out what records there are for 1000 AD. Are there many?' he asked, looking from Doyle to Claire.

Claire nodded. 'Loads. At least, there are for that period. There's bound to be something for that exact year.'

'Like what?' Brendan demanded.

'Maybe something to do with trade,' Desmond suggested mildly.

'*Trade*!' Brendan exploded. 'Buying and selling, and all that rubbish! Couldn't we concentrate on war, or fighting, or something like that? Freedom fighting! Were the Irish independent then, or what?'

'It was about the time of the Vikings, wasn't it, Claire?' Desmond asked.

'Yes.'

Doyle caught Claire's quick glance. Brendan's green eyes were flashing. There were no prizes for guessing what he was going to say.

'That's it, then,' he exclaimed, just as Doyle had expected. 'Can't we compare the Vikings to the British?'

Doyle hesitated. They were all looking at him. It might be a good idea; but then again, it might not. Miss Binchly had warned them not to be too controversial. Maybe she had expected something like this to be suggested.

Claire was shaking her head, and Aisling's face had actually gone white. Desmond voiced their doubts in that quiet, common-sense way he had. 'We'd better steer clear of that,' he said. 'It could get too ....' He hesitated for a moment before finishing, 'Too involved.'

Claire nodded agreement, and Doyle saw her give Aisling a quick smile, as though reassuring her. Maybe a member of Aisling's family was mixed up with

Republican extremists. He didn't know much about her folks.

For that matter, he didn't know much about any of the others. In the year Doyle had been at St Patrick's Primary School, he hadn't mixed much with his class-mates.

When they had moved to Dublin, his parents had decided on St Patrick's because it had a good reputation — and because it was near their workplace. It made life easier. In the mornings, Doyle got a lift in from their house in the suburbs with his father. After school, he went home with his mother, who worked flexitime; her office was one of the first in Dublin to run an after-school club for employees' children, and if she wasn't ready to leave when he finished school, he waited there.

He had been surprised when Miss Binchly put him in charge of the group. She was bound to have noticed that he didn't mix with the others. Either Claire or Desmond would have been the obvious choice.

He looked at Desmond and nodded his agreement. 'You could be right,' he said, ignoring Brendan's glower. 'It could be dodgy. But let's read up about the period around 1000 AD first, anyway, and then decide. We wouldn't have to be exact — just have an idea of the general conditions around that time.' He looked at Claire. 'Where do we start?'

'The reference section in the National Library. There's loads there,' she said, the blue of her eyes sparkling as the light caught her glasses. 'Can you all come on Saturday morning?'

'I should manage.' Doyle nodded. 'But will we get in? Is there not an age limit or anything?'

'We should do, if we get a letter from Miss Binchly,' Desmond told him. 'And Claire knows her way about there. You go —' He hesitated, then corrected himself. 'You went a lot with your father, didn't you, Claire?'

She nodded. 'I still go myself. Sometimes they let me have books on loan for Da. If they won't, he tells me what information he's looking for and I get photocopies if I can find it.' She looked at Doyle. 'Da's a bit of a historian,' she explained, with a quick sideways glance at Desmond.

'Oh, right,' Doyle said. Why can't her father go himself any more? he wondered; but something in the glance she gave Desmond stopped him asking outright. 'Aisling? Brendan? Can you come on Saturday?' he asked.

'I suppose so,' Brendan agreed half-heartedly.

'Not too early, though,' Aisling said.

'About elevenish,' Doyle suggested. 'We'll meet at the door.'

TWO

Desmond and Brendan were waiting when Doyle arrived at the National Library. He glanced curiously at the huge Victorian building; the impressive stone walls looked magnificent in the early-autumn sun. His mother had pointed the building out when they first came to Dublin, but he had never been this close. In fact, he hadn't been across the Liffey to this side of Dublin after that first quick tour of the city; his school was on the north side, and his home was several kilometres out towards the coast, near the Howth Road. Doyle thought of the National Library as a place for great scholars and people like that — not for sixth-class kids researching a project. Claire's father must be a professor or something, he thought.

There was no sign of the girls.

'Nice bike,' Brendan said. 'Why don't you use it for school?'

'My parents aren't keen,' Doyle told him. 'It suits them better if I come in the car.'

'Here's Claire and Aisling,' Desmond put in. 'You'd better padlock the bike.'

'You bet,' Doyle answered, with a grin. There was no way he wanted to risk getting it stolen. He'd only had it since his twelfth birthday, three months back.

'Sorry,' Claire panted as she joined them, with

Aisling lagging behind. 'I had things to do at home. Let's go in.'

She certainly knew her way about. The woman in charge greeted her with a wide smile as she approached the desk. Doyle and the others stood waiting while Claire described the project and explained that they were looking for information about life in Dublin in the year 1000. She was very businesslike, and obviously familiar with the procedure — quite different from Aisling, who was fidgeting nervously beside Doyle.

He hadn't really noticed the others as individuals before. Claire was dark, like himself, with her hair cut in a short, easily managed style. Aisling was thin, and her fair, wavy hair hung loose on her shoulders. She was slightly taller than Claire, about Doyle's and Brendan's height. Desmond was taller than any of them; but then, he was thirteen.

'It's a weird place, isn't it?' Aisling half-whispered, looking back at the mosaic floor they had just crossed.

'Sort of,' Doyle agreed, with a glance at the zodiac signs spread out behind them.

It wasn't so much the surroundings as the atmosphere — although maybe the surroundings contributed to the atmosphere. 'Awe-inspiring' was probably the best way to describe it. There was a sort of hushed silence — not exactly silence, because there was movement and low conversation, but there was a quietness which overrode those sounds. Doyle had felt the same thing in the public library, but not this strongly.

Claire was beckoning to them, and they followed her into the reference section. Shelves of books, old and new, lined the walls. Claire walked towards a table, then stopped beside a shelf of leather-bound volumes, putting out a hand to touch the books lightly with her fingertips, as though she couldn't help herself.

An assistant came forward quickly and asked for the pass which Claire had been given by the woman at the desk; then she indicated a reading-table a little apart from the main area. She glanced, a bit anxiously, at Brendan. They were all wearing school uniform, but Brendan, as usual, somehow managed to be a bit off-putting; his close-cropped ginger hair and earring obviously didn't go down well.

Doyle stared with dismay at the heap of books which appeared before them. They would be here all day! But Claire knew exactly where to look, and, with pencil and paper handy, they ploughed through the pile, exchanging suggestions and ideas in barely audible whispers.

The books they were given weren't that old, Doyle noticed; not like the ones on some of the shelves. Most were newish editions of old works — that is, if something a hundred-odd years old could be called newish. There were some modern editions, too, but they tended to be sort of analyses, written round the original works.

Claire was particularly interested in one of the oldish books. She wrote down something about 'primary sources', and told the others the book was a history of the Irish kings up to the year 1119. Doyle supposed she had figured out who the king of Ireland was in 1000 AD. He leaned over to see the title of the book. It was *The Prophecy of Berchan*.

That fits, Doyle thought with a grin. After all, the millennium hype is full of prophecies of one sort or another.

THREE

'What now?' Brendan asked, as he pushed his way out through the door of the library. He looked over his shoulder. 'I wouldn't fancy spending too much time in there,' he added with a grimace.

'You shouldn't have to,' Claire told him. 'At least, not if we use what we've got. That's up to Doyle.'

Doyle shook his head. 'No, we'll all need to agree. We can discuss it on Monday.'

'Why not now?' Aisling suggested. 'We could go to Paddy's Cove and talk it over, like.'

'Where?' Doyle asked, puzzled. They were well in from the coast; there couldn't be any coves around here, surely? Not that he would know. He was originally from Cork — or had been, before his parents got posted abroad.

Aisling giggled. 'It's a café. Have you never seen it?' she demanded.

He flushed slightly; she hadn't spoken unkindly, but it set him apart from the others, who were true Dubs and knew the area.

'It's on the other side of the river,' Brendan explained. 'Near where one of the old harbours used to be, before the mouth of the river silted up — or whatever it was that stopped ships coming up this far.' He was bending over Doyle's bicycle, fiddling with the padlock. 'I could ride your bike some of the way?' he added.

Doyle hesitated and then handed him the key. Otherwise they might think he was being stand-offish. It should be safe enough. 'OK,' he said, 'but be careful.'

'Great!' Brendan exclaimed. 'See you there, then.'

Doyle opened his mouth to speak, but Brendan shot off down the road in the direction of Nassau Street.

'Don't worry,' Desmond reassured him. 'He'll take good care of it. He spends half his life on a bike — not one as good as that, though!'

Aisling's hazel-flecked eyes were sparkling. 'Let's see if we can get there before him,' she said. 'He'll be going towards O'Connell Bridge. He'll have to cycle along Bachelor's Walk. I know a short cut to the Ha'penny Bridge. If we run, we might make it.'

They didn't, but it was close. Brendan screeched to a halt at the narrow, shabby entrance to the café just as they turned down the lane towards it.

'What did you do?' he asked with a grin, padlocking the bike to a nearby lamppost. 'Swim the river?'

'Something like that,' Desmond laughed.

Desmond isn't even out of breath, Doyle thought, leaning against the wall, panting slightly and with a stitch in his side; it had been a real effort for him to keep up with the others. Desmond had loped ahead, with Aisling following close on his heels. Doyle and Claire had struggled to keep up with them. Not that he was all that sure that Claire had actually been struggling; he had a suspicion that she had deliberately slowed to his pace. He couldn't decide whether to be pleased or annoyed; he didn't like to be patronised. But then again, probably she was being considerate. She seemed to be that sort of person.

'You should be in better shape, with a machine like this to ride,' Brendan declared. 'If it was mine, I'd be cycling every spare minute I had! Here's the key. By the way, your brakes could do with oiling.'

'I usually check it over on a Saturday,' Doyle told him, trying unobtrusively to make sure there were no new marks on the bike. 'I haven't got round to it yet today. Is this Paddy's Cove?'

'Sure is,' Brendan answered, leading the way through the doorway. He stopped to speak to four boys sitting near the door, before making his way to a table by the one window.

'Hi,' one of the boys said to Claire as she passed. 'How's the nu —' He cut off the word as Desmond stopped beside him.

The boy was probably a good year older than Desmond; but Desmond had the advantage when it came to build. His eyes, normally rather dreamy, were like points of steel.

The boy shrugged, then grinned. 'How's the hurling, then, Des?' he asked. 'The match still on next week?'

'Wednesday,' Desmond told him evenly, moving on. 'See you.'

Claire paid no attention at all. She followed Brendan and Aisling to the table by the window and sat down. Only a slight flush on her cheeks suggested that whatever it was the boy had intended to say had upset her. She gave Desmond a small smile as he and Doyle joined them.

'Cokes, is it?' Brendan asked, standing up with a hand outstretched.

'Not for me,' Claire said quickly, as Doyle reached into his pocket and Desmond counted out some change.

Aisling interrupted. 'I'll pay,' she said, producing a ten-pound note with a flourish. She laughed at the expression on Brendan's face. 'I got it from my father this morning,' she explained. 'Might as well spend it.'

'Are you sure?' Doyle asked, staring at the note. His parents might buy him top-of-the-range bikes and the best in computer equipment, but they didn't hand him tenners every week — or any week, for that matter.

'No problem,' Aisling said. 'Da's pretty generous.'

'Four Cokes, then?' Brendan said, raising his eye-brows and lifting the note.

'Five,' Aisling insisted. 'Go on, Claire, the rest are having one.'

Is that why she offered to pay? Doyle wondered. Did she guess that Claire doesn't have any money to spend?

'Sit down, Doyle,' Brendan said, pushing him into a chair. 'You're standing there like an eejit. I'll go for them.'

Doyle laughed self-consciously. He felt a bit like an idiot. He wasn't used to the easy, comradely friendship the others shared. For almost as long as he could remember, his parents had been on the move, usually spending no more than a year — two at the most — in the one place. They had left Ireland when he was six, and he had been to four different schools before they came back to Dublin: one in Luxembourg, one in London, one in Brussels and one up North. It had been interesting, but unsettling. In the early days he had made friends readily, but the wrench each time he moved had made him wary. After a while, he had kept to himself a lot, missing out on things like clubs and games — there was no point in trying to get into a team if you weren't sure you'd be around for the last matches in a league.

He looked out of the window, trying to hide his dis-composure. The four boys who had been at the next table were examining his bike.

'It's OK,' Desmond said quickly. 'They won't touch it. They would've seen Brendan arrive on it, and they're mates of his.'

'Sort of,' Brendan put in, depositing five paper cups of Coke on the table. 'And you must admit, Des, Mikey's a whiz at the hurling. Sorry,' he added, as Coke from one cup slopped onto the table.

Desmond glanced at him quickly. 'What's up?' he asked. 'You look as if you'd seen a ghost!'

Brendan gave a stifled laugh. 'Not exactly,' he said. 'It was that guy at the counter — Liam, his name is. When he saw the tenner, he asked if I wanted *something*. I nearly died! He must have thought I was with Mikey's crowd. Then I could see he realised he'd said the wrong thing, and I tried to pretend I hadn't understood what he meant. I convinced him — I hope.'

'How did he say the wrong thing?' Aisling asked, making no attempt to lower her voice. 'You did want something. You wanted Cokes!'

'Shh!' Brendan hissed. 'He meant drugs, of course, you eejit!'

Doyle glanced over to the counter. A weedy guy was busying himself there, but obviously watching for their reactions to what Brendan was saying. He was probably trying to figure out whether or not Brendan had caught on. It would be better if he thought not.

'*Sláinte*!' Doyle said, raising his voice slightly and lifting the half-empty paper cup. 'No problem, Brendan, there's plenty left. Let's get down to business. Claire's got the notes.'

'Here they are,' Claire said quickly, producing her notebook and slapping it on the table. She opened it. 'This will be what you're on about, Brendan, is it?'

Desmond glanced from Doyle to Claire. 'Good thinking,' he said quietly, as they saw Liam shrug and shake his head to someone in the back room.

Doyle gave a barely perceptible nod. Hopefully the café assistant really was convinced.

FOUR

'So what have we got?' Doyle compared their notes. 'What have we actually found out?'

'That the Irish were trying to get rid of the Vikings!' Brendan contributed smartly. 'We couldn't miss with that,' he insisted.

'And that the Irish were fighting amongst themselves,' Desmond put in, tongue-in-cheek.

'Still are,' Aisling added with a sigh, deadly serious.

Doyle glanced at her. He must be right: she must have some relatives mixed up with Republican extremists. All the more reason to steer clear of that angle. Desmond was right: it could become involved.

'Desmond's idea might be best,' Claire put in. She looked at Brendan. 'It brings in the Viking bit, but it wouldn't be so controversial.'

'You mean about the trade?' Doyle asked.

'Yes. I mean, there's all that about Dublin's economic position in Europe, and how well off people were because of the Vikings' trade links with Europe, and how they'd prospered more than people up North. There is a parallel there, isn't there, with Ireland today?'

Doyle nodded. His parents were always on about that aspect of Ireland's membership of the European Community. 'We can point out how, when Brian Boru captured Dublin from the Vikings, on New Year's Day

1000 AD, it was a major economic centre,' he said.

'Yes,' Claire agreed, her eyes going to the notebook and her fingers fiddling with the legs of her glasses.

'Like, once again we're going into a new millennium on the crest of a wave?' Desmond interrupted.

'Something like that,' Doyle nodded. Seeing Aisling's puzzled expression, he added, 'With things looking really good.'

'Yes, but,' Brendan objected, 'are we going to have to spend hours looking up what sort of goods the Vikings traded?'

'I don't think we need to do that,' Desmond put in. 'After all, it's not like a history project. We're just using the historical bit as a ... a base to start from.'

'Like an introduction?' Aisling said tentatively. 'Then go on to the trade we have with Europe today, and the advantages of being in the EU in the year 2000?'

'That sounds good,' Doyle exclaimed. He looked at Brendan. 'We can bring in your ideas about the Internet — how important modern technology is to the economy as we enter the new millennium.'

Brendan looked somewhat mollified, but he pointedly indicated a note Claire had made. 'What about this, though?' he said. 'From the analysis of that book, *The Prophecy of Berchan*. It says that 1000 AD was the beginning of the end for the Vikings in Ireland. I still think my parallel is best!'

'We get your point,' Desmond said with a laugh, 'but let's leave it at that. *We'd* better not try and prophesy!' He glanced at the weedy-looking assistant — Liam — who had moved to the next table and was intent on wiping it clean.

Liam looked across at them and grinned. 'You kids having a board meeting?' he asked.

'Something like that,' Doyle answered. It might be a

good idea to appear friendly. 'It's a school project on the millennium,' he said. 'We're trying to work out the details.'

'Which millennium?' the assistant asked. 'I thought I heard you mention 1000 AD.'

'We did. We were reading up on that.'

'You should ask that nutter who caused all the trouble over at Trinity last year. He made it sound as if he was the great Brian Boru himself,' Liam joked, as he moved away.

Doyle opened his mouth to ask about the nutter, but an urgent shake of the head from Desmond stopped him. Aisling was biting her lip, as though she was vexed about something; Claire gazed out of the window, concentrating on a dog sniffing at the wheel of his bike.

Brendan quickly brought the conversation back to the assistant's first remark. 'It sounds like this project'll be as boring as a board meeting,' he moaned. 'I still think something on freedom fighters would have been more exciting.'

'I don't know about that,' Desmond said. 'You never know what we might turn up.'

FIVE

'See you Monday,' Claire called as she and Aisling went off together, leaving Brendan and Desmond standing with Doyle as he unlocked his bicycle.

'I hope Claire isn't trying to prove something,' Brendan exclaimed. 'Could be why she suggested the history angle.'

'Don't be stupid!' Desmond said. 'She just knows a lot about that period.'

'Well, she would!' Brendan rejoined with a laugh. 'Wouldn't she?'

Doyle looked from one to the other. What were they on about?

Brendan caught his glance. 'Her father's nuts,' he said.

'He's not,' Desmond put in quietly. 'You know that well, Brendan. He's just a bit mixed up. And he can go for weeks, sometimes months now, with no bother. Perfectly normal.' He rested a hand on the bike and looked directly at Doyle. 'Claire's father — he's my uncle — used to be a lecturer at Trinity,' he explained. 'He wrote an article that the other lecturers, and the media, said was rubbish. Then he had a real downer — clinical depression, the doctor called it — and went a bit funny; he kept trying to put over his point, all the time.'

Was it Claire's father who caused the trouble in

Trinity? Doyle wondered. Thank goodness Desmond
warned me not to ask.

His curiosity got the better of him. 'What was that
guy Liam talking about?' he asked. 'Was it Claire's
father?'

Desmond nodded. 'One of the other lecturers had
written a book,' he said, 'covering a lot of the same
stuff as Uncle Frank's article, but giving a completely
different view. His criticism of Uncle Frank was a bit
much — sneery, like; like he wanted to know had
Uncle Frank been dabbling in New Age magic and
going back in time, to be so sure of his facts. When
Uncle Frank saw the book in the Trinity library, he got
a bit freaked out and started shouting his head off,
saying he should know best — he sort of gave the
impression that he thought he was a reincarnation of
Brian Boru, although I don't think he actually said that.
The same thing happened when he saw the book in
the National Library. So he's banned from both the
National and Trinity.' Desmond shrugged. 'It's old
news now, though,' he added.

This project is getting to be like a minefield, Doyle
thought as he cycled home. I'll have to watch my step.

Hidden problems lay in every direction. There was
Brendan with his extreme opinions on getting the
British out of Ireland, Claire with a father who had
funny ideas about the first millennium, Aisling with
some sort of hang-up about the North ....

What about Desmond? Did he have a problem?

No doubt there would be something. He couldn't be
any different from other people. Not that it showed,
though. Yet he wasn't quite what he seemed — all
quiet common sense and mildness. Doyle thought of
the way he had looked at the Mikey guy — and of
Mikey's instant reaction. Obviously everyone knew

that Desmond wasn't someone to mess with. It was great the way he'd looked out for Claire.

Doyle sighed. His own cousins, five Australian and four American, hardly counted. Not only were they thousands of miles away, but they were also all a good bit older than he was. It would have been great to have someone like Claire living close by. It would have made up for the lack of a brother or sister.

He wondered about being an only child. Maybe his mother had wanted a career rather than a big family. She hadn't come from one, he knew; she had one sister, but no brothers. That was why he had been saddled with the Christian name Doyle: that had been her maiden surname, and her father had wanted it carried on in the family.

It hadn't been a problem when they'd lived abroad. At his school in Brussels, there had been two Scots boys called Graham and Cameron, which apparently were Scots surnames. He had got a few queer looks, though, when he came back to Ireland. Still, people were getting used to it and didn't make it sound as though they were calling him by his surname. But he still felt as though it set him apart somehow.

He sighed, glancing at his watch, and realised with a start that it was almost two o'clock.

Saturday afternoon was family-outing time — a drive up the coast, followed by a meal at some country pub. Doyle grimaced. At his age it was getting to be a bit of a bore. Desmond was probably on some playing-field, practising for the hurling match they had talked about. Brendan might be with him. They would be laughing and shouting and tussling with other boys, smelling of sweat and having fun, the clash of their camáns echoing across the field — with no adults around to cramp their style.

Not that I'd be much good at hurling, Doyle decided, if
all the players are as fast and fit as Desmond and
Brendan. Maybe I should do a bit more cycling and
build up some muscle .... He felt decidedly scrawny
beside Brendan, never mind Desmond.

As he slipped the gears up and pedalled purpose-
fully towards home, someone in a passing bus twisted
round in his seat to look at him. Doyle caught a
glimpse of lank, greasy hair and a thin, spotty face —
and a look of recognition.

Where had he seen that face?

As he watched the bus turn off in the direction of
the fishing harbour, the answer came to him. It was
Liam, the assistant from Paddy's Cove. Maybe he was
going to pick up supplies from one of the fishing-boats
— supplies of what, though?

Doyle had heard his parents talking about some sort
of surveillance being kept on two of the boats at the
harbour. Going back downstairs one night for a book,
he had overheard them talking about their work — and
had stopped behind the door to listen. It wasn't something he should have been listening to, but he had
assumed it was about drug-running and had been
interested.

He grinned, remembering the expression on Brendan's
face after the offer of — as he had put it — 'something'.
Brendan, like most of them, knew the score, but he
very obviously wasn't into anything in that line.

As Doyle turned up the driveway to his house, the
grin became fixed. His mother was standing at the
door, elegantly dressed as usual, while his father was
putting golf clubs into the boot of the car.

Doyle groaned inwardly. Another boring Saturday
afternoon. It was enough to make you turn to drugs!

SIX

Aisling flushed with pleasure as Doyle gave a whistle of appreciation.

'This is fantastic!' he told her, glancing over the print-out she handed him. It was only Monday morning, but everything they had decided on was already carefully detailed. He had felt that Aisling would come up with something half-decent, but this was way above his expectations.

'Do you have a computer, then?' he asked.

'We have a PC, like,' Aisling told him. 'My father gave it to us for Christmas. I share it with my two brothers. My big sister and the baby aren't interested in it,' she added with a giggle.

'That's great,' Doyle said, trying to hide the surprise in his voice. Somehow he hadn't expected her to have a PC. But then, hadn't it been obvious on Saturday that her father wasn't short of money?

'Wouldn't I love a PC,' Claire put in, leaning over Doyle's shoulder to see the print-out. 'I have to make do with Da's old-fashioned word processor. You've made a great job of this, Aisling.'

'My brother helped a bit,' Aisling admitted. 'My father was interested in the project, too.' She looked at Doyle. 'He asked if we'd like to go down to the harbour and see the containers and ships — he's the assistant harbour-master. He said he could even let us see some of the export and import lists.'

'Wow, that's great!' Brendan exclaimed. 'I've always wanted to have a look around those containers.'

'We'd need some sort of pass, wouldn't we?' asked Desmond.

Aisling nodded. Her face was pink with pleasure. She was obviously delighted at being able to contribute so much to the project. 'Da said he was sure the harbour-master would agree.'

'What about next Saturday?' Brendan suggested. 'Could he fix it for then?'

'I'll ask,' Aisling said, with a glance at Doyle. 'Would that be OK?'

'Sounds good,' he told her. It had been a stroke of luck getting her to do the writing-up. Instead of being left out, as he had expected, she was way ahead of the rest of them.

'We'd better cool it a bit,' he added with a grin. 'Miss Binchly looks like she's about to tell us to quiet down.' He took a coin from his pocket and laid it on the table. 'I don't suppose any of you have a Viking coin, have you?' he asked, lowering his voice to quiet the discussion.

Desmond picked up the coin from the table. 'Not me, anyway,' he said. 'There's plenty in the museum, though. What's this, then?' He peered at it. 'A euro! Where did you get this?'

'My father. But it's not valid currency yet. I was thinking about what we read, about Dublin having the only mint in Ireland around 1000 AD, and I wondered if we could get a coin from that period to go with this one. It's dated near enough the 2000 mark, and it'll be used in most of Europe. Anything minted in Dublin around 1000 would have been used on the Continent too — in the Viking settlements, like. That's right, Claire, isn't it?'

Claire nodded and reached for the coin. 'That's cool,' she said, her eyes shining. 'It's the first I've seen.'

'Good thinking, Doyle,' Desmond declared. 'We can get a picture of an old one easy enough. Maybe we could make a rough sort of coin of our own.'

'It wouldn't be the same, though, would it?' Brendan complained. 'I mean, we want the real thing. What if we could find one? There must have been lots hidden away when Dublin was captured on ....' He leant over the print-out. 'On New Year's Day, 1000 AD. That's what people did, isn't it? Buried their treasure till the troubles were over.'

'There's supposed to be a hoard hidden down by the river,' Claire said hesitantly. 'Newly minted coins in a leather bag. Dated 999 AD.'

'Wow! How do you know?' Brendan demanded. 'Did you read it somewhere?'

Claire glanced quickly in Desmond's direction. 'Someone told me once,' she said, flushing slightly.

'Did they say where?'

'Not exactly.'

'Not *exactly*!' Brendan hissed. 'Near enough, like?'

Doyle noticed the frown on Desmond's face. If the 'someone' had been Claire's father, she probably shouldn't have mentioned it. It could be embarrassing. Maybe he had told her that he'd hidden them himself!

There was no stopping Brendan, though. 'Where?' he demanded.

'Near Paddy's Cove,' Claire said reluctantly. 'But it might not be true,' she added quickly, biting her lip and tweaking at the legs of her spectacles.

'We could look,' Brendan declared. 'See if there's a cave or anything on the riverbank. You could be right, Desmond. You never know what we might turn up. Let's go down there after school.'

SEVEN

Doyle didn't want to miss out on anything. And since his mother wouldn't finish work until 5.30, he decided to join in the search. At lunch-time he rang her, to explain that he would be working on their project and would be late arriving for the after-school club. Strictly speaking, that wasn't quite what they were planning, but still .... Claire said she couldn't come; she had shopping to do and had to collect her young brother from day nursery. She seemed genuine enough, not just making excuses. Aisling and Desmond went home to change out of school uniform and to check with their parents.

Brendan didn't bother.

'No point,' he said. 'There won't be anyone in. My mother's out at work.'

'When does your father finish?' Doyle asked.

'He doesn't.' Brendan glanced at him quickly, then added with a shrug, 'What I mean is, he doesn't exist. Or more like, as far as he's concerned, I don't.' He changed the subject abruptly. 'Do you fancy a Coke?'

Doyle nodded. 'Yeah, and I could do with something to eat. I'm starving.'

'We'll get something at the café,' Brendan told him. 'They have great cakes.'

Paddy's Cove was empty when they went in. Liam

gave a quick nod of recognition and a sideways glance at Doyle.

'What was that for?' Brendan asked, as they went over to the table by the window.

'Maybe he was checking to see if it was me he saw on a bike, out Howth way,' Doyle told him.

'How come?'

'He was on a bus going out towards the harbour on Saturday. Must have got on just after we left the café.'

'Maybe they get their fish fresh off the boats,' Brendan said, sniffing appreciatively at the aroma drifting through from the kitchen. 'Wish I had enough money to get one of their fish meals. Mind, I did hear that the boats bring in more than fish!'

'Drugs, like? Where do they get them?' Doyle asked curiously. That tied in with what his parents had been talking about.

'Ships at sea.' Brendan looked at him. 'Where did you get that coin, the euro?'

'From my father. Like I said.'

'Where did he get it?'

'Through his work.'

'What's that, then?'

'He works for Customs.'

'I see.' Brendan gave a whistle. 'Then you'll know a bit about drug-running?'

'Not really. They don't discuss anything at home. At least, not often — and not with me.'

'Does your mother work there, too?'

'Yeah.'

'Wow, you'd need to steer clear of anything like that, then,' Brendan said with a grin. 'Here's the others. Let's get down to the river.'

Y2K

'There's nothing down there,' Desmond pointed out, as they walked along above the river. 'Apart from some drainage pipes.'

Brendan was already climbing across the barrier which separated the pavement from the river and peering down at the stone retaining wall. 'There's some sort of opening,' he said.

'Like I said — a drain,' Desmond told him, practical as ever.

'But they might have put it where there was a natural opening — like a cove — into the shoreline,' Brendan insisted. 'When they made the road. Chances are there would be a small river flowing through the cove into the Liffey.'

'Paddy's Cove?' Aisling suggested tentatively.

'Could be,' Desmond said. 'But if there was anything buried here, it would have been found when the place was built up.'

'Maybe.' Doyle leaned over the railing to pinpoint the position of the opening. He turned and looked over his shoulder. 'Where would the line of the drainage pipes be?' he asked.

Desmond crossed the road and stood considering. 'Through that close, maybe. Then up under the café. Maybe the people who named the café knew a bit about the history of the place — knew that there had been a cove called after someone named Paddy. Maybe the café's built right on top of it.' He grinned. 'I wonder who Paddy was. Let's go round the back of the café and see what's there,' he suggested.

An outhouse at the back straddled what appeared to be the line of the drainage pipes. Beyond that was another road, and beyond that rows of buildings. Before anyone could stop him, Brendan had turned the key which had been left in the outhouse door and slipped inside.

'Brendan!' Desmond hissed, with a quick look at a small window at the back of the café. 'Come out of there! You'll get us into trouble.'

Brendan came back to the door. 'There's nothing in here. Nothing much, anyway. We can't do any harm. The drain does run underneath it, though. I can hear water running, and there's a kind of manhole cover in the floor.' He took a packet of cigarettes from his pocket. 'Might as well have a puff while we're here. Want one, Aisling?'

'Thanks.' Aisling took the proffered cigarette, and Brendan looked questioningly at Doyle.

Desmond obviously didn't smoke, Doyle realised with relief; so it wouldn't be out of order if he refused. He shook his head.

'Fair enough,' Brendan said, producing a lighter — just as Liam appeared around the corner.

'What the blazes are you kids up to?' he shouted. In two strides he had reached Brendan, pushed him aside and slammed the outhouse door. 'This isn't a smoking parlour,' he snarled.

Aisling gave a nervous giggle and moved closer to Doyle.

'Sorry,' Doyle said quickly. 'We didn't mean to pry or anything. It's just ....' He searched for an excuse. 'It's just this project we're doing. Remember, we told you about it? Someone told us that your café was called Paddy's Cove because there was a proper cove here once, and we were following what looks like a culvert put in to drain a stream or river or something.' He stopped for a moment. The rage — and something else which was difficult to define — was dying out of Liam's face. 'We were trying to work out what the place would have looked like a thousand years ago,' he finished lamely.

'That's right,' Desmond put in smartly. 'Do you know who named the café — or anything about the history of the area?'

'No,' Liam said shortly. He reached for the key in the door, turned it, then slipped it into his pocket. 'But you've no right to be here,' he told them.

A voice called from the side door of the café.

'Who is it, Liam? What's going on out there?'

'Just the kids from the school down the road. You know, the millennium kids — the ones I told you about the other day. Doing some project on Y2K.'

'Tell them to clear off, then,' the voice shouted. 'And get back in here pronto. There's customers waiting.'

'Be right there, Boss. OK, you kids, you heard. Get lost! And don't let me catch you nosing round here again.' Liam glared at them, then stood and watched till they were out of sight.

'Wow! What did he get so steamed up about?' Brendan exclaimed. 'I bet they keep their drugs in there.'

Desmond gave him a quick look. 'I thought you said there wasn't anything in there,' he said.

'Not that I could see, like. But there's that cover over where the water was running. They could hide stuff down there.'

'You're letting your imagination run away with you,' Desmond laughed. 'And I think we'd better forget about the Viking hoard — if there ever was such a thing.'

'Probably wasn't,' Brendan retorted. 'Who told Claire, anyway? If it was her father, it's more likely his imagination was running away with him.'

'Maybe not.' Desmond shrugged. 'When he did his research for that article, he might have read something — that there are coins buried around here.'

'Why would anyone hoard coins?' Aisling asked. 'Why not spend them?'

'Maybe they were being saved to buy something,' Brendan suggested, his eyes gleaming. 'Weapons, maybe. There was a sort of guerrilla war going on, didn't Claire say? Like the IRA is — was,' he corrected himself.

'Maybe.' Desmond shrugged. 'But anyway, we'd better forget about trying to find the coins — or anything else,' he warned Brendan.

'Don't worry,' Brendan answered, with a nod towards the café. 'Their secret's safe with me. And anyway, Mikey says they're only into hash. Nothing heavy.'

'It would have been good to find the coins, though,' Aisling put in. 'Should I write up about looking for them, Doyle?'

Doyle considered. 'Maybe not,' he told her. 'We'd have to say where we got the information, and it might be embarrassing for Claire. What do you think, Desmond?'

'Better not. We can make a copy of one in the museum. That'll be easier to explain. It was a good laugh, though.'

It was, too, Doyle thought, as he went off to meet his mother. It certainly beat sitting in the after-school club doing homework. Saturday should be even better. He grinned to himself, remembering the gleam in Brendan's eye. Practical Desmond and enthusiastic Brendan, shy Aisling and intelligent Claire — what a team they made! He laughed aloud.

It was going to be some project!

EIGHT

'Pity you didn't find anything,' Claire told Doyle the following morning, as they waited for Miss Binchly to call the class to order. 'I suppose it was daft even to think we might, when the place has been built up. The coins were probably found centuries ago.'

'Maybe,' Doyle said. 'Maybe your father read about them being found and forgot exactly what he'd read.'

Claire gave him a sharp glance, and he flushed with embarrassment. She would wonder why he thought it was her father who had told her. She hadn't actually said so.

'Sorry — I ... I sort of thought ....' he mumbled. He realised he was making things worse. Now she would guess they had been talking about her father.

Claire shrugged it off. 'It's OK. Everybody knows he can be a bit peculiar,' she said with a sigh. 'I'm used to it. You're probably right, too. The thing is, he can be so convincing — as though he *was* actually there. He knew so many details — what they were for and everything ....' She hesitated and then added, her cheeks slightly pink, 'I checked the records for the incidents he talked about, but I couldn't find anything which tallied. So I guess ....' Her cheeks turned from pink to bright red, and she pushed at her spectacles. 'It sounds a bit mean, I know. But the way things are ....'

'Seems fair enough,' Doyle put in quickly, slightly embarrassed himself by her frankness. He glanced away and added, 'At least you seem to understand him. It's great that you go to the library for him and everything.'

'Well, he is my da.' Claire smiled. 'It doesn't really change anything — the way I feel and that.'

'What were the —' Doyle started to ask about the 'incidents' she had mentioned, but she interrupted him as they were joined by the others.

'At least we've got something out of it,' she declared. 'After Desmond came round to tell me what happened, Da pulled out a box full of bits and pieces an archaeological friend gave him years ago, and he let me have this.' She produced something from her pocket and laid it on the table.

'What is it?' Brendan asked.

'It's a rubbing of an early coin,' Claire told them. 'It shows the two sides.'

Doyle picked up the piece of stiff paper. 'Gosh, well done. That's just what we need.'

He could make out the faint outline of a head on one side. There were letters circling the head — just like on modern coins, he realised with a stab of surprise. A thousand years, and things like that had stayed the same!

The letters were almost worn away, but he managed to sound out what was there. 'S — I — T ....' He looked at Claire.

'"Sitric Rex Dyflin", it says,' she told them. 'I looked it up in one of Da's books. I think the letters on the other side are the name of the man who made the coins.'

Doyle peered at the rubbing. 'What date was the coin?' he asked.

'Da says about 1000 AD. We can check with the

museum, but it must be about then; that was when Sitric was king of Dublin.'

'I thought Brian Boru was king?' Brendan interrupted.

'He was King of Munster, and after 1002 he was High King of all Ireland. And he defeated the Dublin Vikings in 1000 AD, so they were his subjects too,' Claire told him, with just a trace of hesitation.

'High King of *all* Ireland? The whole island, like? A united Ireland ruled from the South?' Brendan raised his eyebrows significantly.

'Yes. At least, sort of. There were lesser kings, but he had authority over them all — I think. But the coin was issued by Sitric.'

'It was sound of your father to let you have this,' Doyle interrupted, cutting Brendan off. 'When we've got everything printed out, Aisling can fit it and the euro in with any other illustrations we have.'

Claire threw him a smile. 'Actually, I think he didn't want to be outdone by your father,' she said. 'I told him about the euro, and that was when he gave me this.'

'Oh, well.' Doyle tried to sound noncommittal. He was only too aware that the fact that he had been given the euro had nothing to do with the project. His father had simply asked if he wanted it, without mentioning the project; he probably didn't even know about that. His mother knew, because of the visit to the café, but she hadn't shown much interest; she wouldn't have mentioned it to his father.

Doyle pictured Claire discussing the project with her father, in spite of everything — telling him about the research in the library and what they had decided. And Aisling, bubbling over with giggling enthusiasm, drawing in the interest of her whole family — to the point that her father had offered to arrange the visit to the harbour. He felt a twinge of regret. It must be great to have that sort of relationship with your parents, he thought. Is it my fault or my parents' that we're not like that?

Aisling caught the glance he had thrown in her direction and smiled at him — a rather sweet smile, almost sympathetic, as though she had read his thoughts. The way he felt must have shown on his face, he realised. He smiled back shyly, then turned quickly as Brendan asked Claire if her father had had anything else interesting. Maybe she would tell them about the 'incidents' she had mentioned.

But Claire shook her head. 'Not that he was willing to show me, anyhow,' she said. 'Normally he's a bit funny about his treasures, so we were lucky to get the coin.' She pushed at her glasses thoughtfully, though, as if there had been something more.

'We're doing pretty well as it is,' Desmond put in quickly. Miss Binchly was calling them to order. 'And I thought I might take my camera down to the harbour — get a photo of a container ship, so we can contrast it with a Norwegian *knorr*. Would that be OK, Aisling? Did your father say if Saturday was on?'

'Yes. He said to go down about eleven o'clock. But what's a *knorr*?'

'A Viking trading-ship.'

'A contrast between warships would be more interesting,' Brendan put in. 'Not to mention weapons.'

Aisling looked at him in alarm. 'There wouldn't be anything like that down at the harbour, would there?'

'No such luck,' Brendan joked. 'Still, it should be good for a laugh.'

NINE

Doyle spun his bicycle to a dramatic halt at exactly ten minutes to eleven on Saturday morning. He had arranged to meet the others at the roundabout at East Wall Road. Desmond was waiting with the two girls, but there was no sign of Brendan.

'Where's Brendan?' he asked.

'Practising for the Tour de France, by the look of it,' Desmond said with a grin as Brendan came into sight, pedalling furiously, weaving in and out of the traffic. They watched, laughing and calling out encouragement, as he covered the last few metres.

'Made it,' he gasped, a foot on the front tyre of his bike to bring it to a halt beside them. 'I got grounded till my bedroom was cleaned out,' he explained. 'I never knew I had so much junk until I started to tidy it away. I'll swop you bikes till we get to the harbour,' he said to Doyle.

'No way,' Doyle laughed. 'Yours doesn't look too safe. You've no brake blocks!'

Brendan shrugged. 'It goes,' he said. 'Mind, though, Mam's beginning to wonder why my trainers are wearing out so quick.' He gave a good-natured grin. 'Let's get moving, anyway. Did you bring your camera, Desmond?'

'Yeah.' Desmond took the camera from his pocket.

'There's ten frames left in the film. That should be enough,' he told them, as he and the girls walked alongside the back-pedalling Doyle and Brendan.

Aisling's father was waiting for them at the harbour. He was a slightly built man with wavy fair hair and quick, darting, hazel-flecked eyes.

'Will your mammy manage all right without you this morning?' he asked, giving Aisling an affectionate smile.

'No problem,' she told him. 'Remember, Deirdre's not working today.'

'Of course. I forgot. It's a job keeping track of my brood,' Mr O'Leary joked, smiling at Doyle. 'You'll be Doyle. Aisling's told me all about you. You're in with a good bunch here. How do you like being back in old Ireland?'

'It's great,' Doyle told him. And it was now, he realised — now that he was one of a group. They were almost like a gang. Aisling must tell her father everything, he thought. My dad wouldn't have a clue what any of the others in school are called.

'I'll give you a quick tour,' Mr O'Leary told them. 'Show you the general layout and where you're not allowed to go. There's practically no movement today, so you should be safe enough. Then you can have a wander about on your own. Just don't go falling into the sea!'

'We'll avoid that,' Desmond said, with his slow smile. 'Is it OK if I take some photographs, Mr O'Leary?'

'I don't see why not, Des. We've nothing to hide — I hope. We're not even having a visit from the Customs' top boys today.' Aisling's father indicated an empty enclosure. 'Anything requiring clearance is locked in there.' He looked at his watch. 'Come on, then. I've got fifteen minutes to spare. We'll go down to the dock first.'

Doyle glanced at the enclosure as they followed Mr O'Leary. His own father, he knew, was one of the 'top boys', one of the investigating team who checked loads and cargoes. Mr O'Leary wasn't likely to know that — unless Brendan had told Aisling that Doyle's father worked for Customs and Excise. Even then, though, he wasn't likely to know his position; Doyle hadn't said what his father actually did.

'Wow! Aren't they huge? They'd each hold at least two Viking trading-ships,' Brendan exclaimed, as they stood by the harbour wall looking at the containers waiting to be loaded onto ships. Mr O'Leary had gone off, leaving them to look around.

'It must have been more interesting then, though,' Claire said. 'I mean, you could have seen exactly what was being loaded or unloaded from the ships. We don't know what's in the containers.'

'Da said he could let us have copies of some of the slips listing the contents,' Aisling reminded them. 'It would make it more real. We can ask him.'

'He's busy just now,' Desmond pointed out, adjusting the camera to take a photograph. 'He's talking to those men over there.'

He nodded towards Mr O'Leary and two other men, who had just appeared from behind the nearest container, only a few metres from the harbour wall. Focusing on the container, he pressed the release button, just as one of the men looked up.

'It's that Liam from Paddy's Cove, isn't it?' Brendan exclaimed in surprise.

The other man — an older man — looked over quickly at the sound of Liam's name.

'Who are they?' they heard him ask. 'What's with the photographs?'

'That's the Y2Kids, Joe,' Liam joked. The three men started walking towards where Doyle and the others stood. 'Kids from one of the schools. They hold their board meetings in the café where I have the part-time job. They're doing some sort of school project about the millennium.' He turned to Aisling's father. 'Have they roped you in to help?'

Mr O'Leary laughed. 'Aisling there is my daughter, so I got permission for them to have a look around.'

'The wee girl with the fair hair, obviously,' the man called Joe said, giving Aisling a long, considering look. 'You couldn't deny that one.'

The men laughed. Then, as they passed with a friendly nod, Joe tripped, knocking against Desmond. The camera fell to the ground.

'Oh, sorry — that was clumsy of me.' The man bent and recovered the camera before Desmond could move. He examined it for a moment before handing it back. 'Still, no harm done. It's intact. Carry on with the good work,' he said, moving on.

'What's that Liam doing here, I wonder?' Brendan said, once they were out of earshot. He looked at Doyle. 'Visiting both harbours in one week!'

'He said something about his job in the café being part-time,' Claire pointed out, moving on ahead to catch up with Desmond and Aisling. 'Maybe his proper job is as a driver.'

'So what was he doing in a bus?' Brendan mumbled.

Doyle shrugged. 'Who knows?' he said lightly. But he frowned. Maybe he should mention Liam to his parents. After all, he knew — or suspected — that Paddy's Cove supplied drugs. And he knew about the surveillance — but then, he wasn't supposed to know about that. And it wasn't the sort of thing he could bring up casually with his father.

What does it matter, anyway? he thought. After all, as Brendan had said, it was only hash. It was even legal in some countries — not that his parents agreed with that.

Liam and the other man — Joe — drove off in a white van about half an hour later. Doyle and the others, making their way slowly back towards the main gate, stopped while Desmond focused the camera out towards the sea. Mr O'Leary, watching from his office, called to them and came out to join them. He pointed out the line of the shore as it might have been, centuries back.

'Try to imagine it without the harbour walls,' he told them. 'But anyway, you should be able to get a copy of a picture of it as it was before the walls were built. Have you taken a photograph of it as it is now, for comparison? Try one from a bit over to the left. Have you many frames left on the film?'

Desmond glanced at the numbering. 'That's funny,' he exclaimed. 'It's not showing anything!'

Mr O'Leary took the camera and had a close look. 'There was a film in it, was there?' he asked.

'Definitely. There were ten frames left. I checked.' Desmond frowned, fiddling with the camera.

Doyle couldn't help the giggle which rose in his throat. Desmond would find it hard to believe he had forgotten to put a film in — even if he had. He was always so self-assured, even a bit smug. Sometimes he seemed much more than a few months older than the rest of them.

But Claire was backing him up. 'That's right,' she

told him. 'You took the fourteenth one the other day. Of Mam and the baby.'

'There's no film in there now,' Aisling's father said. He opened the camera carefully to show the empty cavity.

'It must have fallen out,' Brendan exclaimed. 'When that man knocked against you. I'll go back and look.'

Mr O'Leary glanced at his watch. 'I'll have a look,' he said. 'I have some checking to do over there anyway. If it's there, I'll give it to Aisling tonight. But here ....' He took a ten-pound note from his pocket. 'I was going to give you this, Aisling, for ice-cream or whatever it is you kids buy. It should stretch to another film as well.'

'That's really good of you. Are you sure?' Desmond asked politely.

'Quite.' Mr O'Leary smiled. 'And there's a big container ship due in next Saturday, if you want to come and get some photos of an actual unloading. You might want repeats of the shots you took today, too; even if I find your film, the last few frames will probably be ruined. Now I'll have to be getting on,' he told them, moving off. 'See you next week, then.'

It wasn't until Doyle had left the others and was half-way home that he remembered hearing a click as the man called Joe examined the camera. Had he deliberately taken the film out?

But why would he do that?

And what was his connection with that Liam?

I must remember to say it to Brendan when we meet up tomorrow, he thought. It was a pity he had to get back home for the afternoon. But Claire hadn't been free either, so the treats from Mr O'Leary's tenner had to wait till the next day. In a way, Doyle was glad; that would be more fun than the usual dull Sunday outing with his parents.

He cycled along slowly, reviewing the morning in his mind, trying to picture the harbour as it might have been a thousand years ago. A thousand years — a whole millennium .... The mind boggles, he thought with a laugh.

Then he stopped as the realisation struck him. The harbour wouldn't have been *there*. They'd forgotten that. Hadn't Brendan mentioned something about the river silting up? So maybe the ships — and they had been a lot smaller back then, anyway — would have come right up the river before that happened. Maybe into the centre of the city ....

Up as far as Paddy's Cove?

Doyle's heart raced at the thought, and his front wheel struck the edge of the kerb as his attention wandered. He wobbled dangerously back onto the road as a car sped past, the horn blasting.

Steadying himself, he cycled on, but his mind was racing ahead.

Just suppose ships had been unloaded in the vicinity of Paddy's Cove? Or even been loaded — with what? Newly minted coins, perhaps?

Doyle laughed aloud at himself and the ideas which were running mad in his head. His imagination was inclined to run away with itself.

But somewhere in the background, a thought was niggling at him.

Maybe Claire's father was right. Just maybe there were coins hidden there.

TEN

Aisling hadn't been too happy about going back to Paddy's Cove, but the boys had laughed away her fears. It wasn't as if they had done any damage or caused any trouble, they pointed out. And anyway, the Liam guy had been quite friendly when he saw them down at the harbour; he obviously didn't hold a grudge.

As it turned out, Liam wasn't there. Sunday was probably his day off, they decided.

The café wasn't too busy. A few teenagers were crowded in one corner, playing a video game; at the table where Mikey and his pals had been, two elderly men were reading a Sunday paper. Aisling giggled and nudged Doyle, drawing his attention to the fact that the paper was divided between them: one had the sports page, the other the news section. Doyle grinned, wondering if they swapped sections or if they had separate interests.

Desmond had bought a film for his camera that had the cost of processing included in the price. As they sat around the window table, he rather apologetically produced the change from the tenner. The film had been a smart idea, Doyle thought, but the money that was left wasn't going to go far between five of them.

Not at all daunted, Claire picked it up and went to the counter in a very businesslike way. She gave her order politely, but with a firmness which had the rest of them choking back giggles.

'Please may I have two cans of Coke, five paper cups, two of the sticky buns and a knife,' she asked.

'Well ....' The man hesitated, a hand half-outstretched towards a can of Coke, as though not entirely pleased. 'It's an unusual request, like,' he said. Then, as Claire looked at him coolly in feigned surprise, he grinned. 'OK, then. Here. I've got to admire your nerve!'

As she moved away with the tray, he called her back. 'You forgot the knife, Madam,' he said, tongue-in-cheek.

'Oh, yes. Thank you,' Claire said, taking it and placing it neatly on the tray. 'We'll need that.'

Desmond was looking slightly embarrassed, but Aisling and Brendan were almost under the table with hysterics. Doyle grinned broadly as Claire laid the tray down. She divided the buns into five equal portions — no easy task — and then proceeded to share out the two cans of Coke. The man at the counter, highly amused, winked at whoever it was who did the cooking in the kitchen area. You really had to hand it to Claire!

As Brendan savoured his portion of bun, he glanced at the camera lying beside Desmond's cup. 'Pity about losing the photos of the harbour,' he said. 'I don't suppose your father found the film, did he, Aisling?'

Aisling shook her head. 'No luck. He looked all around, but there was no sign of it anywhere. You're sure there was one in it, are you?' she asked Desmond.

'Positive.'

'You don't think —' Doyle began, but Brendan interrupted him.

'It won't matter. We can get better photos next week,' he pointed out. 'Which reminds me — did anyone remember that the harbour was further up the river a thousand years ago?'

'It occurred to me,' Doyle told him.

Desmond nodded. 'I thought of it too,' he said. 'There are drawings of early Dublin, but they're from a bit later than 1000 AD. Like Wood Quay — that was thirteenth-century, I think. We might have to make do with illustrations of that, maybe showing ships unloading — you know, like the sort of sketchy black-and-white drawings in the history books.'

'That would be cool,' Aisling declared. 'It would match the ones you're going to get on Saturday. They'd give a good balance to my print-out.'

Or we might find drawings of ships loading, Doyle thought. He couldn't get the picture of a ship taking on a cargo of newly minted coins out of his mind. It occurred to him, too, that there just might be old maps or something like that in the Customs House. Should he say anything? Maybe not. If he did, the others would take it for granted that his father would get copies for them — and he didn't know how his father would react if he asked. Anyway, Doyle thought with something like relief, anything like that would be in a library or a museum; it would be easy enough to see.

Brendan was leaning forward, elbows on the table, his chin cupped in his hands, his eyes shining. 'Hey, Des,' he exclaimed. 'Do you remember the stories that old fella on the riverbank used to tell us?'

Desmond's face lit up. 'Janey, yes. I'd forgotten. It's ages ago.'

'Who?' Aisling demanded. 'What stories?'

'Old Jock,' Brendan told her. 'Remember? He used to sit on that bench by the river, just a bit down from here.'

'Oh, him. But he was sometimes ....'

'Inebriated,' Desmond finished with a grin.

'To put it mildly,' Brendan said. 'Remember the time you stopped him falling over the wall?'

'The day your hurley landed in the middle of the road!' Desmond laughed. He turned to Doyle and the girls. 'It was when we were in fourth class. We were on our way to hurling practice and Old Jock asked to see our camáns. He said he'd been a top shinty player in Scotland. Brendan told him shinty was rubbish compared to hurling, and that the Irish could beat the Scots any day.'

'Well, I didn't know then that they're practically the same thing,' Brendan retorted. 'But you should have seen Old Jock's face!' he told the others. 'He was livid. Grabbed my stick and started to show us his swing.' He choked with laughter, remembering. 'The stick went flying across the road, and he staggered against the wall between the pavement and the river — just as a garda car passed. Desmond grabbed at him, and they both nearly went over — with Old Jock's dog barking and leaping round them. Then we saw the guards getting out of the car, and we ran for it!'

'I was grounded for a week,' Desmond said. 'My parents weren't impressed.'

Doyle glanced at him quickly. It was the first time he had heard Desmond mention his parents. How had they known about the incident, if he and Brendan had run off? If the guards recognised him, Doyle thought, his father must be quite well-known.

Claire's laughter was a bit strained, Doyle noticed. For a moment he wondered why. Then he realised what was bothering her: they were all laughing at Old Jock in much the same way that Mikey and his pals had been about to make fun of her father. Desmond obviously hadn't thought of that. Doyle moved uncomfortably in his seat and glanced over at the two elderly men reading their paper. If his and Aisling's amusement over the shared newspaper had been obvious, he realised with a stab of guilt, it could have been hurtful in the same way. At the very least, it had been rude.

Aisling must have been thinking the same thing; she glanced at the men and then at Doyle. She gave a small shrug, as though to indicate that the harm was done and it was best ignored. She turned to Brendan and Desmond, though, and interrupted their reminiscing.

'I thought Old Jock was nice,' she said. 'When he wasn't drunk. And I liked his dog,' she added.

'Too right,' Brendan agreed. 'The dog was fantastic. A black-and-white collie,' he told Doyle and Claire. 'Pity it got run over. Old Jock was heartbroken. He was sound. It was what happened with the hurling stick that was funny — not really him,' he added, with a look at Aisling's face.

Desmond nodded. 'Lots of people used to stop and talk to him,' he said. 'And even when he did have a bit too much drink on him, the gardaí never arrested him or anything. They'd just take him home.'

'And he told great stories,' Brendan added.

'What kind?' Claire asked. Doyle suddenly realised that she hadn't been at the same school when they were in fourth class. Maybe they'd only moved to the area after her father's trouble.

'That's the thing,' said Brendan. 'It just struck me when we were talking about the harbour. Old Jock said he'd worked on the roads around here, years ago, and he used to go on about an old harbour or a jetty or something — he said they'd seen the remains of it. They found an old axe-head, too. Old Jock said it must have come from Scotland — something to do with its shape. It was sort of double-sided. But apparently the firm he was working for told the workers to keep their mouths shut. They didn't want the archaeologists coming in and holding up the job. I think he kept the axe-head.'

'When did he tell you that?' Claire's eyes had widened with interest. 'How long ago?'

Brendan looked at Desmond. 'Three years, like?'

'Could be.'

'Does he still come down to the river?' Claire asked.

'He was ancient!' Aisling said. 'He's probably dead.'

'No, he's not,' said Desmond.

'How do you know?' Brendan demanded. 'He's never about any more.'

'My father and some of the others sometimes call in and see him. Take him a drink and have a chat. He's what they call "a real character".'

'Call in where?'

'That Home for old people, across the river. I think he's about eighty-five now.'

'Could we go and see him?' Claire asked. Her voice was hoarse with excitement, and Doyle wondered suddenly if the 'incidents' she had mentioned were connected in any way with an old harbour.

'I suppose so,' Desmond said slowly, looking round to see their reactions. 'We could explain about the project. If there was a harbour or something like that around here, that would give us an extra edge to the project. It'd be better than using what's already in the history books.'

Brendan shuddered. 'I don't like those places for old people. My ma's father ended up in one. He had Alzheimer's. I hated visiting,' he admitted. 'Anyway, five of us would be too many.'

'That's a point.' Desmond considered. 'I'll ask Da and see what he thinks. Would you come, Doyle?'

'Sure.' There was no way he was going to miss hearing about that old harbour, Doyle decided. And if Claire was on to something, he wanted to be in at the beginning.

ELEVEN

When Doyle got home, his parents were entertaining some of the neighbours. Feeling in the way, he decided it was as good a time as any to do something positive about his body. Ten minutes in front of the bathroom mirror had convinced him that sitting in front of his computer all day wasn't doing anything for him. He was as tall as Brendan; if he concentrated on building up his muscles he might manage to look as sturdy, he reckoned. Cycling seemed to be the answer; Desmond had said Brendan spent half his life on a bicycle. And Doyle's mother was always on at him to get out into the fresh air — to put colour in his cheeks, she said. Maybe that was the reason for Brendan's ruddy complexion. Doyle peered into the mirror, running a finger down his pale face. She could be right, cycling might do something for the pallor. This was as good a time as any to start.

He decided to cycle along the coast. There was time before it got dark. He could go out towards the fishing harbour, over by the lighthouse. There might be another angle on the coastline that Desmond could photograph. The marina might be worth a visit, too.

By six o'clock he was on his way, dressed in denim shorts and a T-shirt. On his mother's orders, a rolled-up waterproof jacket was stuffed into his school backpack, along with a can of Coke and some chocolate biscuits. There was a west wind and he bowled along easily, slipping down side-streets to avoid the mainstream traffic.

It was cold by the fishing harbour's sea wall. The waves pounded against it, then broke into long smooth drifts which merged with the calm surface of the harbour waters. Doyle shivered, wishing he had worn his fleece.

The whole place reeked of fish. He cycled slowly away from the smell, towards the lighthouse, wondering if the public was allowed inside. There was no one about whom he felt he could ask. Perhaps his father could take him someday. After all, the harbour officials around here were bound to know the Customs men. The trouble was, his parents never suggested anything like that.

He stood for a while looking back at the lines of brightly coloured fishing-boats — blue ones, blue and white, red, blue and red, or black. Some were a bit flashy. He preferred the smaller red ones, and one particular black one with an old-fashioned wooden cabin.

Were the ones which were under surveillance here?

Doyle considered, giving his imagination free rein. If he was looking for a ship running drugs, which one would he choose? The one with the high prow, reflecting bright blue and white onto the water, with expensive-looking gear on deck? Was that too obvious? Or would the owner use that fact as a cover? But maybe drug barons preferred something less conspicuous. His eye rested on the black boat. What about that one? No; he couldn't imagine it somewhere out at sea, alongside a large yacht, with two or three fishermen looking over their shoulders as a man in a white suit, smoking a large cigar, oversaw the loading of packets of cocaine ....

He laughed aloud at the picture in his mind. It probably wasn't like that at all. He'd love to know, though. Maybe I should ask Dad, he thought. Maybe my parents just don't think I'm interested, because I never ask.

Aisling didn't seem to have any problems with her father. Even Claire, in spite of her father's illness, had some sort of rapport with him. And Desmond was going to consult his father about the visit to the Home .... Why couldn't it be as easy for him?

Doyle sighed, the laughter gone, and turned his bike in the direction of the marina. But he would ask about the lighthouse, he decided. Then his father might realise that he was interested in what went on at the harbours. He might even ask about any old records or maps in the Customs House ....

A movement on the deck of the black fishing-boat caught his eye, interrupting his thoughts. Someone had come out of the small wooden cabin — someone whose stance was familiar; a tall, broad boy.

The boy turned to speak to someone inside the cabin, and Doyle recognised his face instantly.

It was Desmond.

What was he doing there?

TWELVE

There probably wouldn't have been any harm in going back to the fishing-boats and speaking to Desmond, Doyle thought, as he cycled down a long wooden-slatted jetty to look at the yachts moored in the marina. It might be Desmond's father's boat; or perhaps it belonged to an uncle. Maybe they would have invited him on deck, let him look over the vessel. That would have been interesting. Doyle felt like kicking himself for not thinking about it at the time and going straight there. Why was he so backward?

The atmosphere at the marina was completely different from that among the fishing-boats. For a start, there was no smell — at least, not of fish; but a man was varnishing the hull of a small dinghy turned bottom-up on the shore. Doyle sniffed. The varnish smelt a bit like the glue he used for his collection of model ships. He cycled slowly back onto the road, towards a grassy bank which ran alongside it; he parked his bike and scrambled halfway up. He spread his jacket on the ground and opened his can of Coke. This was as good a place as any to drink it. There was a good view of the sea, and he was sheltered from the cold October wind. Black clouds were piling up, he noticed, as though there was going to be rain; it was just as well he had brought his jacket.

But he noticed that the man varnishing the dinghy didn't seem concerned. Maybe it was quick-drying varnish. It would need to be — double-quick, at that, Doyle thought with a grin, as a curtain of light rain moved slowly across the surface of the sea. But perhaps the shower would pass them by.

He sat there for a while, the near-familiar smell of varnish giving him a sense of well-being as he drank the Coke and ate his chocolate biscuits. There was more movement here than around the fishing-boats. Some distance out to sea, a line of buoys marked what was obviously a racing-course; a number of small sailing-boats were tacking to the left and right of them. Doyle watched idly as beams were swung across and crew members shifted from side to side, at times seeming to lean perilously near to the foam-flecked waves. It was surprising the boats didn't keel over.

A fairly large yacht, making its way slowly towards the marina, turned sharply to avoid the course. Doyle pulled his knees up to his chest and leaned forward slightly to watch its progress. Several people were waiting on shore, near a berth, and a man on the yacht waved to them. As the vessel drew near the berth, a man detached himself from the group and stood ready to catch the mooring-rope. Doyle sat upright, his eye-lids half-closed against the glare off the water, hardly believing what he saw.

It was hard to believe that, in a city of one and a half million people, he should see two he knew in the space of an hour. But there was no mistaking the weedy-looking man standing poised, an arm outstretched to catch the rope snaking across the space between the yacht and the jetty.

There was something incongruous about the two sightings. Doyle would have been less surprised if he had seen the two people in the opposite places. Desmond spending a Sunday afternoon at the marina, watching the yachts and helping with the mooring — maybe getting the odd tip — would have made sense; and Liam on the fishing-boats would have confirmed Doyle's suspicions.

But the other way round?

It had been fishing-boats his parents had been talking about in connection with the surveillance. He was sure of that.

And Liam wasn't just a casual helper. The crew of the yacht had greeted him, and, as Doyle watched, he went on board.

Doyle frowned, and the unresolved question which had been at the back of his mind all week came to the surface. Should he talk to his father about Paddy's Cove, about the fact that drug-dealers worked from there — and about the fact that he had seen Liam at the main harbour, on his way down here, and now actually here?

If he did, what would that make him? A grass? No; to be a grass, he would need to have been in direct contact with the dealers. A sneak, though, or a spy? Or just a good citizen?

But his father wouldn't take kindly to the fact that he had been eavesdropping and knew about the surveillance. Maybe he could bring up the subject of drugs casually, without letting that slip .... Hardly; he'd probably just get a lecture on the dangers of drug-taking. They would need to have an adult conversation about drugs and drug-dealing. And there wasn't much chance of that; they didn't have that kind of relationship.

And anyway, he didn't have any proof that Liam *was* involved in anything. It would be easy enough for Liam to deny the offer he'd made to Brendan in the café.

There was something else, too — something that

was niggling at the back of Doyle's mind, but which he didn't want to think about. Even if his suspicions were right, he thought, there was no way he could get the police or the Customs involved. He would lose the others' acceptance forever. In his mind's eye he saw Aisling's open, happy face, flushed with pleasure at being able to contribute so much to the project; he thought of her enthusiasm, her carefree lifestyle with the baby, her brothers and older sister, her busy mother and doting father ....

He shrugged, trying to dismiss the problem. As Brendan had said, it was only hash. He watched as Liam disappeared below the yacht's deck. It's none of my business anyway, he thought, getting up to leave.

The man varnishing the dinghy looked up as Doyle passed. 'See you,' he said.

'See you,' Doyle replied absent-mindedly.

He grinned to himself as he cycled off. That had been a stupid thing to say; there was hardly a chance in a million that he'd ever see that man again.

But the man's accent, even in those two words, had had a familiar ring.

Where had he heard it before?

THIRTEEN

The next morning, on the drive to school, Doyle brought up the question of a visit to the lighthouse.

His father threw him a sharp glance. 'When were you down at the harbour?' he asked.

'Yesterday. In the evening.'

'I see.' Mr Whelan accelerated in order to overtake the car in front. 'Have you noticed how few people seem to be in any hurry here?' he commented, drawing in to their own side of the road once more without giving Doyle a direct answer.

'Mm.' Doyle hesitated, then decided not to be side-tracked. He had to make a start somewhere. 'Would it be possible? To look around the lighthouse?' he persisted.

'What's the sudden interest?'

'It just looks fascinating.'

'Well, I'll have a word,' his father said. 'See if it's possible. Not this week, though,' he added quickly, as they drew up outside the school. 'Maybe sometime after next weekend. Would that do?'

'Great.' Should I ask now about any old Customs records? Doyle wondered. Would that be pushing my luck?

Just then, Brendan shot past the car on his bike. On the spur of the moment, Doyle asked, instead, 'Could I bring someone?'

His father's surprise was obvious. 'Well, yes — I suppose so.' He gave Doyle a quick smile. 'The boy on the bike?'

'Yes.' Doyle flushed. He'd never been in the habit of asking people home. Somehow he'd always felt it would be an inconvenience to his parents. Seeing Brendan, though, it had occurred to him that he might like to come. He could cycle out. Then, after that, he might come often. They could go for spins together. That way, maybe Doyle would still spend time with him and the others once the project was finished.

His father seemed to approve of the idea of including Brendan. Maybe it's partly my fault that we never talk, after all, Doyle thought. Maybe I don't try hard enough.

'Thanks,' he said, meeting his father's eyes. 'It would be fun.'

'Fine. Just let me get this weekend over first, though,' his father told him. 'Then we'll arrange something. I'd enjoy it myself. It's a long time since I did anything like that. Off you go, now,' he said, as Doyle slipped out of the car.

Doyle had missed the opportunity to ask about the Customs records, but he still felt happy — and more confident that he would be able to ask later.

He didn't say anything to Brendan about a visit to the lighthouse. It would be better to wait until his father made the arrangements, he decided — just to be sure.

But by the middle of the week he was sure that Brendan would accept the invitation. They spent some time together during lunch breaks, and after school on Wednesday Doyle went along to the flat where Brendan lived with his mother. She was out at work, but his grandmother was there. They had mugs of tea and some home-made pancakes before Doyle had to leave to catch his lift home.

Brendan decided it would be quicker if they used his bike. Which they did — with Doyle perched perilously on the saddle behind Brendan. They passed Aisling and Claire pushing buggies along the pavement. Aisling shrieked after them, 'Don't kill yourselves before Saturday!'

There was a hiss of leather against rubber, and, before Doyle realised that Brendan's foot had gone out towards the front wheel, he found himself astride the back tyre.

'Sorry.' Brendan grinned. 'I should have warned you I was going to stop. You OK?' he asked, as the girls drew level.

'Fine,' Doyle told him, with a grimace and a sideways glance towards Claire and Aisling.

'That's one way of getting off,' Aisling giggled. 'You'd better watch out the guards don't see the two of you on the bike.'

'We're safe enough,' Brendan retorted. 'Where are you two off to?'

'Just taking the kids out of the way for a while,' Claire told him. She looked at Doyle. 'Desmond rang me. He's arranged the visit to Old Jock for tomorrow after school. But Aisling can't come.'

'Oh.' Doyle was surprised at his own disappointment. He had taken it for granted that Aisling would be going. 'Why not?' he asked, looking at her.

'My mother's got an appointment at the hospital. Deirdre's working, so I've to go along and watch Maeve here,' she told him.

'Too bad,' Brendan said. 'Why has your mother got to go to the hospital? She's not ill, is she?'

The two girls exchanged glances. 'No,' Aisling told him. 'It's just a routine scan.'

'You mean there's *another* one!' Brendan exclaimed,

with a quick look at the toddler in the buggy.

Aisling's cheeks flushed pink. 'Yes,' she said defiantly.

'That'll make six,' Brendan declared.

'So?' she retorted.

Doyle was mystified. What on earth were they talking about? Had Mrs O'Leary had to get six scans at the hospital, or what? Maybe he'd better not ask, in case he said the wrong thing.

But his curiosity got the better of him. 'Six what?' he asked.

Claire gave a giggle, and Doyle flushed. Brendan laughed outright. 'Six kids in the family, you eejit,' he said. 'Aisling's mother's going to have another baby!'

'Oh.' Doyle felt the flush deepen and knew his cheeks had turned from pink to crimson. He didn't know much about babies — especially about women having them. 'Is that good?' he asked. Six seemed an awful lot.

Aisling gave him one of her smiles. 'It's all right,' she said with a shrug. 'Ma's OK about it. Da's over the moon. But then, he doesn't have to carry it.'

'Carry it? Carry what?' Doyle asked.

Brendan was bent double. 'Wow,' he gasped, 'are you ignorant!'

Claire was trying not to laugh, but Aisling was looking at Doyle with sympathy. This is how she feels when she gets things wrong, he realised.

'Like for the nine months,' she said gently.

'Oh. Yes — of course. Sorry.' Doyle tried hard to regain his composure. He laughed it off with a shrug. 'Brendan's right, I'm a bit of an eejit sometimes.'

'Don't worry,' Claire said airily. 'We all get things wrong sometimes.'

'Tell me about it!' Aisling said, grimacing.

They all looked at her in surprise. This was the first

time she had said anything about her slowness in picking things up.

Brendan went straight in, making no pretence of not knowing what she meant. 'Best just to say nothing. If you do put your foot in it, cover it up somehow, if you can — or laugh it off, like Doyle did.'

'Or ask straight out,' Claire suggested.

'Don't be shy about it,' Doyle added, surprising himself with the gentleness of his tone.

'Thanks.' Aisling looked at him and blushed. Brendan and Claire exchanged knowing grins.

'Maeve's getting restless,' Aisling said hurriedly. 'We'd better get moving, Claire.'

'And we'd better get a move on,' Brendan told Doyle, indicating the saddle of his bicycle. 'Your mother will be sending out a search party.'

'Right. Off we go.'

Doyle waved jauntily as the bike wobbled along the road. I'd never have guessed that a school project could make such a difference to my life, he thought, as they slithered to a halt outside the Customs House.

'See you!' Brendan called as he shot off.

'See you!' Doyle responded happily.

FOURTEEN

'What project is that, then?' Doyle's father asked as they ate their evening meal. 'Is it to do with the light-house?'

Doyle shook his head as he bypassed the vegetables in his Chinese take-away. 'It's on the millenniums, the first and the second,' he said. 'At least that's the angle we're taking. It has to do with the harbour, though — and Brendan said that this old man Jock knew a bit about where the old harbours were. He's in a Home and we're going to visit him. That's why I thought it would be easier if I took my bike tomorrow. It'll save Mum waiting, since I don't know how long we'll be.'

'"Millennia" is probably more correct,' his mother corrected him automatically. 'And who's Brendan?'

'The boy whose house I went to this afternoon. Dad saw him this morning.'

'I see.' Mrs Whelan raised her eyebrows at her husband.

Doyle began to wonder if he'd pressed some magic button or something to get this much attention. It didn't last long, though. His mother turned away almost immediately, to ask his father's advice on arranging the ladies' golf tournament. Doyle bit his lip in vexation. He hadn't asked about the Customs records yet. He'd really need to do it tonight.

He waited until there was a pause in the conversation. 'About the project —' he began.

'What about it, Doyle?' his mother asked sharply. 'Can't you see I'm trying to arrange a team for next week?'

'I'm sorry,' he mumbled. 'But this will only take a minute.'

'Can't it wait?'

'I really need to tell the others tomorrow.' He looked hopefully at his father.

'Right, then. You have my attention. What do you need to tell the others that's so important?' His father looked at him seriously, but there was a gleam in his eye. Doyle wasn't sure whether it was of amusement or interest.

He flushed slightly and asked, 'Do you know if there are any old records in the Customs House? Something that would show the positions of earlier harbours — or even show how the river silted up over the years?'

'Well, now, that's your mother's department,' Mr Whelan said, leaning back in his chair and smiling at his wife, as though challenging her to play her part in the unusual conversation.

'How?' Doyle looked from one to the other.

'I'm in charge of the archive section,' his mother told him. 'Such as it is. I thought you knew.'

How could I know? Doyle thought. They've never discussed it with me before. But, then again, I've never asked.

'Are there many records?' he queried.

'I'm not sure if there's anything from that far back,' she said. 'Anything of real historical interest will be in Trinity Library or the National Museum. There are some maps, though,' she added thoughtfully. 'I could

get you photocopies of the earliest ones we've got.
Would that do?'

'Oh, cool! Would you?' Doyle beamed. It didn't
really matter if they couldn't use them. It was the
principle that mattered — just knowing that his
parents were interested enough to help, and being able
to say so to the others. Even Brendan's grandmother
had been interested. She had chattered on for ages
about what Brendan called 'the olden times'.

'And can I take my bike tomorrow?' he asked
hopefully.

'All right. But don't be too late home. Mrs Healey
and her husband are coming round for drinks in the
evening. I'll want to get the dinner over early. Now, do
you want some of that trifle that's in the fridge?'

'Yes, please.'

'Seamus?'

'No, thanks. I'll give it a miss and get on with my
paperwork, if we're entertaining again tomorrow,' Mr
Whelan told her.

As Doyle passed through the kitchen, he heard his
father say, 'I thought you were worried about his lack
of enthusiasm. There's plenty there tonight!'

Is that how they see me? Doyle wondered. Colourless
and flat — a sort of cardboard cut-out?

And what about Brendan and the others? What did
they think of him — apart from the 'eejit' bit?

Doyle grinned. Maybe he'd better have a read of
that booklet his mother had 'accidentally' left lying
about — the one titled 'Sex Education for Boys'. He
wasn't going to have Brendan call him ignorant again!

FIFTEEN

'You can leave your bike at my house if you like, Doyle,' Claire suggested after school the next day. 'The Home's not far along the road once we cross the bridge.'

'That's grand. Thanks.'

Doyle had been going to ask Desmond, but he hadn't been given an opening. Not that it mattered, since Desmond lived on the same street as Claire. There was something odd about him, though. He offered practically no information about his parents or home life. And his attitude discouraged questions, somehow; Doyle hadn't mentioned seeing him on the boat. Not that Des was stand-offish; it was just as though he didn't want to talk about his parents, about what they did. Brendan would know. Maybe I'll ask him, Doyle thought. That'd probably be better than letting my imagination take over.

There was no sign of Claire's father as he wheeled his bicycle round the side of the house. Doyle had hoped at least to catch a glimpse of him; but Claire had gone into the house and come back out fairly quickly, with a handful of biscuits. Her mother waved to them both from a window as they left to meet Desmond.

Doyle wondered what Claire's father felt about the project, and how much he knew about the old harbours.

Claire would know if anything Old Jock told them tallied with what her father believed. But then, Old Jock's stories probably wouldn't go that far back.

Claire was certainly on a high as they approached the Home. Her eyes were bright as though with some inner excitement. Desmond glanced at her once or twice, then — with a glance towards Doyle — warned her, 'Don't get your hopes up. Even if Jock says something about an old harbour there, it might not mean anything. It wouldn't mean ....'

He stopped, and Doyle realised that they must have been discussing something earlier — something which Desmond didn't want to mention in front of him. For a moment he felt awkward and in the way.

But Claire was quite forthright. 'It's all right,' she said. 'I don't mind talking about it with Doyle. He's one of us now. And, anyway, you understand a bit about my father, don't you?' she asked, turning to Doyle.

Doyle nodded. He hadn't thought about Desmond telling her what he had said. But it explained her frankness when she had talked about the 'incidents'; she must have known then. He smiled at her, his heart warmed by being included as one of them. The sense of belonging was completely new to him.

'Are you hoping you'll find out something that would explain your father's stories?' he asked.

'I suppose so. I'm just not sure. I just have this funny feeling inside me,' Claire explained, as they turned up the driveway to the Home.

'Well, here's hoping,' Desmond said quietly, opening the door. 'In we go.'

Doyle realised suddenly that what they were doing had become more than a school project. There was something deeper involved — something more meaningful.

The thought was a bit scary, and a shiver ran down his spine. Something of Claire's sense of anticipation gripped him.

Where was it all going to lead?

The building was an old Victorian mansion. The tiled vestibule led into a large, high-ceilinged hall; at the far end, a carved banister marked the stairway's sweep upwards to the first floor. Both the stairs and the floor were carpeted, and comfortable chairs were arranged around the walls. Through an open door Doyle could hear the drone of a television set, and the smell of baking wafted through the building. The overall impression was of comfort and cosiness.

He stared around in surprise, not sure what he had expected, but knowing it wasn't this. Something more like a hospital, probably, he thought. Since he'd had as little association with elderly people as with babies, he had never had any reason to visit a place like this. His father's parents were in Australia; his mother's father had died ten years before, and her mother had gone to live with Doyle's aunt in America. He was beginning to realise how narrow his upbringing had been.

Desmond and Claire seemed quite at ease. They nodded to the people seated nearby, and Claire went over to speak to a small, white-haired woman, while Desmond looked around for someone in authority. Claire obviously knew the woman: she knelt for a moment or two by the chair, bringing her face down to the level of the woman's eyes, and touched her hand gently before she moved away, much as she had touched the books in the library. The woman had worn a rather blank expression when they came in, but now her face was alight.

'Mrs Maguire,' Claire explained quietly, as she rejoined Doyle. 'She used to be a neighbour.'

Desmond reappeared, followed by one of the nuns who helped to run the Home.

'I'm Sister Catherine,' she said, leading them across the hall. 'Jock's over here in the alcove. He's been looking forward to this since your father telephoned,' she told Desmond.

'It's all right for us to be here, is it?' Desmond asked politely.

'Indeed, yes. Just look how everyone in the hall has perked up. Jock will be kept busy answering questions all evening! It's not often anyone gets a visit from a group of youngsters.' She swept them across to the alcove, where a man was watching their progress with interest. 'Here's Frank Kiely's son and his friends, Jock,' she said, as he stood up. She nodded at two chairs and pulled another over from the wall. 'Sit yourselves down,' she told them. 'I'll leave you with him.'

'It was good of you to see us, Mr MacDonald,' Desmond said, shaking the proffered hand. 'This is Claire and Doyle.'

'The pleasure's mine, lad,' Old Jock replied, offering his hand to Claire and Doyle in turn. 'But as I remember, it was always "Old Jock" down by the river,' he added, with a gleam of mischief in the shrewd brown eyes and a wink in Doyle's direction. 'Make it Jock — I'm not so keen on the "old" bit.'

Doyle suppressed a grin as Desmond's cheeks flushed pink. It took a lot to shake Des's composure. This was a different man from the old fella, often the worse for drink, whom he had stopped to chat to as a kid.

For some reason, Doyle had had a mental picture of Jock as tall and gaunt, slightly bent, with matted grey hair. He was practically the opposite. He was short, not all that much taller than Desmond — about five foot nine, if that — and wiry, rather than thin; and there was no obvious grey in his dark-brown hair. In fact, with his brown eyes and ruddy cheeks he looked a bit like a robin, and the way he cocked his head to one side when he was listening added to that impression. Doyle had noticed that when Sister Catherine spoke to him, she had raised her voice a little and spoken clearly and precisely. Maybe Jock's a little deaf, Doyle thought. Would Desmond know?

Jock was laughing at Desmond's embarrassment, teasing him, maybe remembering how he had been teased. 'You've two fine pals here,' he said. 'What happened to the two you used to hang about with? A red-haired lad, an imp if ever there was one, and the bonnie lass with the sweet smile — timid, she was, though.'

'Aisling had to mind her sister,' Desmond told him. 'And Brendan ....' He hesitated. 'Brendan couldn't make it.'

Jock gave him a quick glance. 'Aye,' he said, 'sensitive underneath the brashness. A good lad. Seen the worst side of places like this, has he?' He looked round the hall, where most of the elderly had once more lapsed into their own worlds, some nodding off to sleep, while others gazed vacantly into space. 'It's mostly the drugs they have to take,' he said. 'Leaves them a bit dozy. I steer clear of any sort of pills, myself.'

'A typical Scotsman,' Sister Catherine interrupted with a smile, as she appeared with a tray. 'Obstinate as they come. Here's that Irn-Bru you had in your room, Jock, with three glasses — and a mug of tea for yourself.' She smiled at Claire as she laid the tray down on a nearby table. 'I know it's probably sexist to expect you to do the honours just because you're the only female,' she laughed. 'But I'm a bit old-fashioned.'

'You're a right good soul,' Jock told her as she

moved away. He reached for a chocolate biscuit from the plate beside the glasses. 'Help yourselves,' he said, picking up the mug. 'This is just what I need to wet my whistle before I answer your questions. School project, isn't it?'

Doyle realised with a start that he had almost forgotten the purpose of their visit, he had been so taken up with Jock as a person. Claire's eyes were flashing, though, as she poured out the Irn-Bru.

'We're hoping you'll be able to give us some information,' she said. 'About the old harbour — and anything you know about what might have happened there in the past,' she added hopefully.

It was a long shot, Doyle thought. But it might just come off.

SIXTEEN

Jock sat for a moment, considering. When he did start to speak, it was with some hesitation. 'Those stories I used to spin you,' he said, looking directly at Desmond, 'they were well embroidered.'

Doyle's heart sank, and Claire's disappointment was obvious. 'You mean you made them up!' she exclaimed.

Jock gave her a quick, penetrating look. 'Some of them,' he told her frankly. 'But, mind you, even those had a thread of truth. I always wove them round some fact or other.'

Desmond grinned. 'Like when Brendan was egging you on about the Viking invasions and what they did to people?'

'Aye, I exaggerated a bittie there,' Jock laughed. 'Though, mind you, they had some nasty habits. You didn't take me seriously, anyway. I knew that.'

'We were only kids,' Desmond excused himself.

'Aye. And good kids at that. Your chats lifted my spirits many a day.'

'But what about the old harbour?' Claire asked, a finger easing the legs of her spectacles. 'Did you really see it? And how old would it be?'

'Aye, I saw what certainly looked like the remains of harbour walls — or maybe just a jetty. I didn't see enough to be sure. Early-Viking-style, they were. That would put them back to — what? Nine hundred and something, maybe?'

'How did you know?' Doyle asked curiously. 'I mean, that they were Viking.'

'Oh, I'd done a spell of construction work up in the northern isles, in Orkney. There's some good examples there, and I had a passing interest. Took note of some of the building features.'

'Didn't you tell anyone?' Claire put in. 'That you knew what the ruins were?'

'Only the Gaffer, lass. You see, we were working on a bonus system. It was back in the late 30s; I came over from Scotland with a construction firm, and we were working hell for leather — if you'll pardon the expression — to get the work finished in the set time. Too quickly to do the job well,' he added thoughtfully. 'In one section, we ran out of drainage pipes, and the Gaffer made do with old oil drums! He couldn't get clear of that area fast enough. Said it gave him the creeps. I pointed out that the oil drums would rust over time, but he shrugged it off. There was good money riding on getting the work finished on schedule.'

'Would the ruins you found not have been worth something?' Desmond asked.

'Just a delay while the boffins nosed about,' Jock told him. 'When I pointed them out to the Gaffer, he told us all pretty sharply to keep our mouths shut and get the lot covered pronto. Later I wondered if I should tell the authorities. But — well, who was going to listen to me? By that time the drink had me in its grip. What would have been the point?'

He stopped for a moment or two, reaching for another biscuit and draining what remained in his mug. 'In a way, I'm sorry I didn't push the Gaffer into doing something about it back in the 30s,' he told them. 'The place was interesting. The drains had been put in years before, and we were renewing them. With all the digging, there's no saying what we might have found. There had obviously been some sort of cove there, with a small river flowing through it.'

'Paddy's Cove, like?' Claire asked.

'Could be. No one seems to know just why the café nearby is called that. For all we know, the good man Patrick himself might have had a cell around there — maybe even hid in a cave when he was fleeing from slavery. I did hear that there was a monastery some-where around there at one time.' Jock grinned. 'There's a story in that. But it's not stories you'll be wanting, but facts.'

'It needs to be,' Claire told him.

'That's about it, then,' Jock said. 'You're welcome to use it, for what it's worth. There's no proof, though. Only my word.'

'What about the axe-head?' Doyle asked, looking at Desmond.

'Yes,' Desmond said quickly. 'Remember, you told Brendan and me that you found one — and that it was old. Was that at the same time? Or was that just one of your fancies?' he added with a grin.

'No, that was a genuine axe-head,' Jock told them. 'A Lochaber axe, at that. Fearsome weapons, they were — an axe-head and a hook, back to back, with a long handle. This one's in my room.' He laughed. 'Gives the good Sister the shudders every time she sees it! You've got a camera, have you?'

Doyle nodded. 'Des has.'

'Bring it round, then, and you can photograph it.'

'Thanks. That would be great. Did you say *Lochaber* axe?' Desmond asked. 'Like the place where that

Hurling-Shinty International was played a couple of years ago?'

'Aye, and where I was born and bred. That's what made me so interested in the axe-head. And, funnily enough, I read an article only a few years ago about the place where I found it. The article was one of those real gems that turn up now and again. It was a wee bit controversial, but the writer seemed to know what he was on about. It was maybe based on legend rather than authentic records, though, since there was some controversy over it at Trinity.' He glanced at Claire, whose eyes had widened. 'But then, to my mind, there must be a fact around which the legend is built. And if there was any truth in what that writer wrote, it would explain how the axe got here — along with the men who brought it, God rest their souls.'

Jock stopped for a moment. 'Maybe the Gaffer knew something — or sensed it,' he went on thoughtfully, as though talking to himself. 'He was a superstitious beggar, anyway. Maybe it wasn't so much the money as what we might find that had him rushing us all on.'

Claire was leaning forward. 'Find what?' she asked breathlessly.

Doyle felt his pulse quicken as he caught her excitement. Was this the 'incident' her father had described? Had that article been written by him?

SEVENTEEN

Jock settled back in his chair and stayed silent for a long moment, as though he was gathering his thoughts.

'You'll all know about the Vikings, the Northmen from Scandinavia?' he said at last. 'How they had overrun a good part of western Europe — Ireland in particular — by the end of the tenth century?'

Claire nodded. 'Yes,' she told him. 'We've read up on that since we started this project. We know how Dublin was a Viking settlement, like.'

'Aye, I can see you're a smart one,' Jock told her with an approving glance. 'And what about Brian Boru?'

She nodded again. 'A bit. How he was King of Munster and then High King of all Ireland.'

'And how he played a big part in getting Ireland back for the Irish,' Doyle put in.

'Aye, he did that,' Jock agreed. 'I can see you lot are going to make a good job of this project.'

'But what's the connection with the axe-head?' Desmond asked, as Claire moved restlessly in her chair. 'And with the place you come from — Lochaber?'

'Well, you'll not know much about Scottish history,' Jock said, 'so I'll just sketch in the background. In the early days there was plenty of to-ing and fro-ing between Ireland and Scotland. There were disputes and there were alliances, and one of these alliances, according to

the article I read, was between Kenneth III of Scotland
and the King of Leinster — this would be between, say,
980 and 1005. This is where the story gets interesting,'
he told them, with a glance at their eager faces. 'As you
probably know, the great Brian Boru had defeated the
Leinstermen in his bid to be High King of all Ireland —
in the 980s, maybe, I'm not sure. At any rate, Leinster
was one of the last of the kingdoms of Ireland to
acknowledge his authority. Even when they finally did
surrender, that didn't end the rivalry between them
and Brian Boru. And he still had the Viking settlement
of Dublin — Dyflin, it was called then — to conquer.

'Then, in 998, Dyflin capitulates. He's almost there;
the High Kingship is almost within his grasp. But a year
later — problems! Word comes from Dyflin: the Vikings
are having second thoughts about acknowledging his
authority. Brian Boru decides to teach them a lesson.
As the year draws to an end, he musters his men and
marches towards Dyflin.'

Doyle leaned forward in his seat as Jock stopped for
a moment to rest his voice. 'But what happened?' he
asked. 'Where does the axe-head come into it?'

'Well,' Jock said, reaching for the bottle of Irn-Bru
and pouring some into his empty mug, 'according to
the article I read, the King of Leinster had been
waiting for an opportunity to get his own back on
Brian Boru, and he saw his chance. What followed is a
bit controversial, though. The writer wasn't able to
back up his claims.'

Doyle glanced at Claire. Her eyes didn't move from
Jock's face. She was waiting avidly for what he had to
tell them. The project was forgotten; what mattered
now was whether the story had any relevance to her
father. How much does she know about what was in
the article? wondered Doyle.

'What did he claim?' Desmond asked quietly. 'Was it that Scotsmen fought against Brian Boru at the famous battle on New Year's Day 1000?'

Jock glanced at him, startled, then nodded. 'That was the gist of it — that the Leinstermen had arranged for Scotsmen to fight.'

'But ...?' Desmond picked up on his answer.

Jock shrugged his slight shoulders. 'Some of them were Highlanders from Lochaber. They came over for the fight — they were aye ready for a fight, that lot! — but when they arrived and realised which side they were expected to support, things changed. It went against the grain for them to fight for the Vikings against Brian Boru; he was a Gael, like the Highlanders, and the Viking was a common enemy. The western Scots, no less than the Irish, were desperate to get rid of the Vikings; why would they help them keep their hold on Ireland? Not all the gold coins in the world were worth that!'

'Gold coins?' Doyle asked, his eyes widening. Beside him, he sensed rather than saw the almost-imperceptible nod of Claire's head. So there is some connection, he thought, his heart quickening with excitement.

Jock's shrewd brown eyes moved from face to face. 'You know about the coins?' he asked.

'We heard something about newly minted coins having been buried somewhere,' Desmond told him.

'Aye, and like as not they still are,' Jock said. 'When I read that article, I could have cursed the Gaffer — well, I probably did. The gold and silver in that payment would have been worth far more than any bonus.'

'Payment?' Doyle asked.

'Aye, that was the deal. The Vikings had plundered Irish gold and silver and minted it into coins which could be used throughout Europe. A sack of those coins was promised to the Scots in return for their help.'

'So what happened?' Doyle urged him on. 'After they came over?'

'Well, according to the article, everything was well planned. They landed on the opposite side of the Liffey from the Viking settlement of Dyflin, at a place where a large stream from a hill lough ran into the Liffey to form a cove — a cove with cliffs riddled with caves going well back into the rocks. This was where they hid. The plan was that, when Brian Boru attacked the settlement, they would come in against him from behind.'

'Were they paid before the attack?' Desmond asked.

'Oh, yes. You bet,' Jock told him, with a touch of humour.

'And what happened?' Doyle put in. 'Did they fight?'

Jock shrugged. 'The Lowlanders among them did, but the men from Lochaber threw down their weapons — their broadswords, their targes, their Lochaber axes — and refused.'

'Targes?' Desmond asked.

'Sort of shields, like,' Claire said, without taking her eyes off Jock.

'And then?'

'The Vikings weren't too pleased, as you'd suppose. However, they reached an agreement. But the Vikings weren't going to send the Highlanders off to join the other side and spill the beans. There were a hundred of the Lochaber men, and they agreed to remain in one of the caves, sealed in by the Vikings, until the battle was over.'

'That was risky,' Desmond exclaimed.

'They didn't think so,' Jock told him. 'They took the sack of gold and silver coins in with them, to make sure the Lowlanders would get them out after the battle!'

'Good thinking!' Doyle laughed.

'But the coins are still there,' Claire said quietly, positively.

'And the men too,' Jock replied. 'God rest their souls.'

'You mean ...?' Doyle stared at him.

'Aye. According to this article, there was a landslide. What with the hundreds — maybe thousands — of men fighting in the area, and the fact that the land was riddled with caves and would have been weak anyway, the hillside came down. They were trapped — lost.'

'There's nothing in the records,' Claire said into the silence that followed.

'No, lass,' Jock agreed. 'So I believe. But then, it was a small incident beside the sacking of Dublin; the chroniclers of the time could easily have overlooked it.'

'So how did the man who wrote the article know?' Desmond asked.

'Hearsay, possibly,' Jock said. 'The Lowlanders from Scotland would have taken the tale home, told how the Highlanders had died; then it might have been written down in local records which lay unread over the centuries. These things happen.'

'Then someone finds them,' Claire said, 'and begins to make connections. That's what research is about. But with nothing in the official records, nothing could be proved.'

'That happens,' Jock agreed. 'But anyway, there you have it. Not much use for your project, though, if it's facts you need. Still, the axe-head is upstairs, and if you bring your camera round you're welcome to take a photograph.'

'Sounds good,' Desmond said. 'And thank you very much for everything.'

'Thank *you*.' Jock grinned, showing a row of strong

brown teeth. 'It's a while since I've had such an attentive audience, I can tell you. Here's Sister Catherine coming to chase you out. Call in any time.'

'Bye,' Claire said quietly. 'And thank you.' She crossed the room to speak to Mrs Maguire.

Doyle glanced at Desmond as they waited by the door. 'Would that have been the article Claire's father wrote?' he asked.

'I think it must have been,' Desmond answered with a frown. 'I just hope it doesn't get her hopes up too much. I mean, what else is there to go on? The Lochaber axe could have been left there any time, by anyone, for all we know! It would be different if the coins had been found.'

Or could be found, Doyle thought with a sigh.

If only ....

EIGHTEEN

Doyle couldn't stop himself asking. 'Will you tell your father?' he asked Claire, as they walked back along the road towards her house.

'About the axe-head and the Viking ruins? I don't know. He knows about the rest,' she said. 'That was the article he wrote.' She flushed slightly. 'When he gave me the rubbing, I saw printed pages in the box with it. Later, when he was out, I had a quick read.' The flush deepened. 'I knew about the incident anyway,' she excused herself. 'He used to talk about it a lot before ... well, before he got a bit better.' She gave a deep sigh. 'If only Jock had said all this back then — when Da wrote it — people might have believed him, and he wouldn't have got ill.'

'The axe-head could have been left there at any time,' Desmond pointed out.

Claire nodded. 'I know, but there was the ruined harbour, or jetty — or whatever it was. Someone might have managed to get permission to excavate there .... I'm not sure whether to say anything or not. Mam was a bit worried anyway, when I talked about the project and Da gave me the coin-rubbing, in case it brought it all back and his mind started to wander again. I felt a bit guilty; I hadn't thought about that.' She looked at Desmond. 'Would you ask Uncle Frank what he thinks?'

'Good idea,' Desmond told her reassuringly. 'Don't worry about it.'

Listening to them, Doyle felt a stab of envy. They had a great relationship; Desmond was more like a big brother to Claire than a cousin. But then, maybe that was what it was like to have a cousin about the same age. He wouldn't know .... For a moment or two he felt awkward, left out.

When they reached Claire's house, her father was standing by the gate. 'Hi, Da,' Claire greeted him. 'This is Doyle. It's his bike that's up the side of the house.'

'So your ma said.' Professor Kiely gave Doyle an intense look, as though trying to figure him out, then smiled. 'Hello there,' he said, in a rather detached voice. 'Nice to meet you.'

'Hi.' Doyle wondered what else to say, but Professor Kiely was already moving away, a plastic bucket full of withered flowers in his hand.

Claire hesitated for just a moment, then turned to Doyle with a smile. 'Are you coming in?' she asked.

Doyle glanced towards the window; Mrs Kiely was smiling out at them. He would have liked to go in and meet them all, but something in Claire's slight hesitation made him feel that she might find it awkward. Probably it would have been easier if he hadn't known about the Professor's problem.

Not that the Professor appeared to be, as Brendan had rather rudely put it, 'nuts'. He looked quite normal. He was about the same age as Doyle's father, with a bit of a stoop and greying hair. Doyle had been very conscious, though, of the penetrating gaze of the grey eyes. And anyway, he decided, if he did go in, the Professor was more likely to ask where they had been — and that would be awkward if Claire wasn't sure she wanted to mention what they had found out.

Doyle glanced at his watch. It was later than he had thought, anyway. 'Sorry,' he said regretfully, 'I can't. My mother's expecting visitors and wanted to get dinner over early. I'll have to go now.'

'Too bad,' she said. 'Next time. See you tomorrow.'

'See you,' Desmond called, opening the door and walking in.

Des is probably as much at home in Claire's house as in his own, Doyle thought, cycling towards the Howth road. He might even stay and have dinner with Claire and her family ....

He sighed. There was a good chance that his own parents would have eaten and he would be having his meal on his own.

Still, he comforted himself, the visit to Jock had gone well. No wonder Desmond's father — whatever he did — thought of Jock as a 'real character'. And, as Brendan had said, he was great at the stories.

Doyle increased his speed, pushing himself and the bicycle against a head wind, invigorated by the fresh air and exertion. By the time he reached home, his cheeks were glowing and his eyes sparkling.

His mother glanced at him approvingly as he entered the kitchen. 'The good Irish air is beginning to take effect at last,' she said. 'That's a fine colour in your cheeks.'

'It's making me hungry, too,' Doyle told her. 'What's for dinner?'

'It's there, by the microwave; just pop it in when you're ready. Your father and I have eaten. He had some paperwork to do before the Healeys arrive. Oh, by the way,' she added, indicating a large envelope on the table, 'I got photocopies of some old maps for you. There wasn't anything going right back, but there is an illustration showing Dublin Bay as it might have been about 1000 AD, if that's any use.' She pulled a sheaf of papers out of the envelope. 'There's some notes, too,' she added. 'A quick summary of how conditions on the river have changed in relation to the increasing size of ships over the years. Would they be useful?'

'Great! Sound. Thanks.' Doyle beamed. 'Is this the earliest map?' he asked, picking one up. 'Gosh, look — it's even got the names of places on it! And there's a stream there — coming down from a hill lough! That's really great. Thanks.'

Mrs Whelan laughed. 'Well, I wasn't expecting so much enthusiasm. This is certainly worth the trouble of getting them for you.' She let her arm rest round his shoulders briefly and gave him a quick hug before awkwardly moving away.

Doyle smiled at her shyly. He would have liked to hug her back, but they weren't that kind of family. They didn't hug each other much. And he was coming up to thirteen, too old for that sort of thing.

He realised suddenly, though, that his mother was like him — or, rather, he was like her. They had the same diffident nature when it came to close relationships. The thought gave him a warm glow, a sense of belonging.

He remembered the agonies he had gone through two years before; he had been convinced that he was so different from his parents that he must be adopted or something. He had smothered the thought only by doing some surreptitious snooping among his parents' papers. He couldn't be at ease until he found his birth certificate, until he had the proof of his birth in black and white. He had felt guilty about what he was doing; but he couldn't ask outright to see the certificate because of his doubts. He understood only too well how Claire had felt about checking up on her father!

'It's a good feeling, isn't it?' his mother said, as she filled a plate with canapés.

'Great,' Doyle answered. He knew she was talking more about what was happening to them as a family than about his enthusiasm over the project. Maybe, though, the changes were happening because of the enthusiasm .... Good old Miss Binchly, he thought as he looked down at the maps. If she only knew!

'Could I take my dinner up to my room?' he asked. 'I want to look at the maps with my magnifying glass. And could I have some of those?' he added, pointing to the canapés.

'Just a few, then,' his mother answered in her usual brisk manner. 'And don't leave any dirty dishes up-stairs. Maybe you could look into the drawing-room for a minute or two later, though, and say hello to the Healeys — just to be polite. Then you can excuse your-self to do your homework.'

'Will do.' Doyle put his heated meal on a tray and then, as he left the kitchen, heaped a plate with canapés. If he was quick, he would be gone before his mother noticed how many he had taken. With the envelope tucked firmly under his arm, he went up to his room.

He couldn't wait to examine the earliest of the maps. That river winding down from the hill lough seemed to be exactly where they would expect from what Jock had told them.

Claire's father must have been right, he thought.

If only they could match the euro with one of those newly minted Viking coins! It would be like having a bridge between the two millennia.

NINETEEN

'How did the storytelling go?' Brendan asked Doyle the next morning, as they kicked a football about the playground.

'Great,' Doyle told him. 'Just like you said, he's great at telling stories.' He glanced around the playground, but there was no sign of Claire. 'Jock had read Claire's father's article, the one where it says about newly minted coins! That was what Jock told us about. He said the coins would have been somewhere near the place where he found the axe-head. Told us about Highlanders from Scotland getting trapped in caves and dying there.'

'He never told me anything like that!' Brendan exclaimed. 'How did Claire take it?'

'She was quite excited, I think, but she stayed pretty cool. She didn't say anything to Jock about her father having written the article.'

'Is she going to tell her father? I mean, about the ruins and the axe-head?'

'She wasn't sure. Desmond was going to ask his father whether she should. Is he Claire's father's brother?'

'Yeah, I guess so. I don't know their families all that well, though.'

Doyle opened his mouth to ask about Desmond's

father, but Brendan got in first. 'What was the Home like?' he asked. 'Were there lots of funny old people?'

'No.' Doyle laughed. 'It was dead smart, actually. Not like I expected. It was like a proper home, almost. Real comfortable — and the Sister we saw was nice. She and Jock seemed to be great pals.'

'Maybe I should have come,' Brendan said, obviously regretting having missed out on something. 'I wanted to see Old Jock, right enough, but ever since I used to have to visit my granda those places have given me the creeps.'

'That one wouldn't,' Doyle assured him. 'And Jock asked Desmond about you. Said you were ....' He stopped, trying to remember the exact words. '"A good lad" — that was it,' he said with a grin.

Brendan laughed, and his face brightened with pleasure. 'He remembered me, like?'

'Yes. And Aisling. We're to go back and take a photo of the axe-head. You could go then. If I don't go, there won't be too many. I think he'd like to see you.'

'I might, at that. Were the other old people ... all right?' Brendan asked. 'You know — in the head.'

'I think so. Some were a bit dozy, but Jock said that was the drugs they were on. They certainly weren't crazy or anything.'

Brendan bit his lip. 'It's just that my granda went right off the deep end sometimes. Really crazy, like. I was terrified when he was like that. Mind, I was only seven. I suppose it would be different now.'

'It would be,' Doyle reassured him. 'And anyway, there's nothing like that there.'

'Do you have grandparents?' Brendan asked curiously.

'In Australia, and a grandmother in America. I don't really know them.'

'That's tough.' Brendan looked at him with genuine

sympathy. 'I wouldn't be without Gran for anything, and I can remember some good times with Granda before he got ill.'

'Your gran's pretty special,' Doyle told him. 'I really liked her — and I can still taste those pancakes she makes!'

'She thought you were "a very nice boy",' Brendan said, in a prim voice which set them both falling about with laughter.

'What's the joke?' Aisling asked, as she and Claire cut across the playground.

'My gran thinks Doyle is a very nice boy,' Brendan told them.

'So he is,' Aisling said, with a puzzled look.

'Well, we know *you* think so!' Brendan teased, winking at Claire.

Aisling blushed crimson, and Doyle gave Brendan a friendly push. Then he remembered the maps.

'Wait till you see the old maps my mother got!' he told them.

'From the Customs House, like?' Brendan asked, his eyes widening.

Doyle nodded.

'Deadly!' Brendan exclaimed. Then, as he spotted Desmond coming in the school gates, he called, 'Hey, Des, hurry up! Doyle's got some brilliant maps to show us. His mother got them.'

'Cool,' Desmond said. 'Your parents have been great.'

Doyle flushed with pleasure. It was hard to believe that life could improve so much in so short a time.

TWENTY

'I have to go in to work this afternoon,' Doyle's mother told him at breakfast the next morning. 'Will you be all right on your own?'

'Sure. Are you working too, Dad?' Doyle asked.

His father looked up from his newspaper. 'Yes,' he said. 'I'll have to go in earlier than your mother, though.'

'Oh, I didn't realise that,' Mrs Whelan said. 'I wasn't going to use my car.'

'Afraid you'll have to. There's a van or something which needs clearance at the freight harbour. We said we'd do that about two o'clock. Before ....' Mr Whelan glanced at Doyle and left the sentence unfinished.

'We're going to the harbour this morning,' Doyle told him.

'Who are "we"?' his mother asked.

Doyle grinned. 'The Y2Kids,' he said.

'The *who*?' his father exclaimed.

'It's just a name someone called us,' Doyle explained with a laugh. 'The five of us on the project.'

'Oh, the project. Is what's-his-name — Brendan, is it — included?'

'Yes. And Desmond and Claire and Aisling.'

'That reminds me,' Mr Whelan said. 'I had a word about the lighthouse visit. What about next Sunday? Have you mentioned it to your friend?'

'Not yet. I was sort of waiting until it was definite, like,' Doyle said guiltily.

His father seemed unperturbed by Doyle's doubts. 'You'd better check with him, then,' was all he said.

'The lighthouse?' Mrs Whelan raised her eyebrows.

'I wanted to look around the lighthouse at the fishing harbour,' Doyle told her. 'Dad said he'd try and fix it.'

'*Next* week,' his father emphasised, looking at his wife.

She nodded, as though acknowledging something unspoken. 'It's all go for you these days, Doyle,' she commented. 'I hope your schoolwork's not suffering.'

'The project *is* my schoolwork,' Doyle pointed out, putting his mug and cereal plate in the dishwasher. 'I'll just clean my bike before I meet the others.'

At five minutes to eleven, Brendan joined Doyle at the main entrance to the harbour. They had all decided to go along the Liffey and try to picture the riverbank as it was in the oldest of the photocopied maps. That might help them to pinpoint the location of what appeared to be a cove on the map — near the café, hopefully. But that would come after the visit to the harbour.

Claire and Desmond arrived five minutes later. There was no sign of Aisling. After ten minutes, they decided that she must have gone on ahead.

'We'd better go in,' Claire said. 'Over to her father's office. Maybe she thought that was where we were meeting. You know how she gets mixed up sometimes.'

As they passed the office window, they could see Mr O'Leary sitting at his desk. His head was in his hands, and his fingers were working frantically through his hair.

At the door, Desmond hesitated, glancing at the others. 'It didn't look like she was there,' he said in a low voice.

'Maybe something's wrong at home,' Brendan suggested. 'Her mother might be sick. Mr O'Leary looks worried.'

'We'll have to ask,' Claire said.

Desmond nodded, knocked at the door and opened it. Mr O'Leary looked up quickly, something like alarm on his face.

'It's just us,' Desmond said quickly. 'We were looking for Aisling. Is something wrong, Mr O'Leary?'

Something very obviously is, Doyle thought. Aisling's father was ashen, and the lines on his face were etched deep into his cheeks. For a moment he had looked almost terrified.

But he quickly pulled himself together and answered Desmond. 'No, everything's all right, Des. Nothing to worry about. But I forgot all about you lot coming! We'll have to cancel the plans, I'm afraid. Will next week do instead? I'm really sorry.'

'That's OK. Next week is fine,' Desmond told him. He hesitated for a moment, then asked, 'Is Aisling at home? Is it all right if we ring her?'

Mr O'Leary's expression didn't change, but his face got even paler. 'I'm afraid she won't be there,' he said. 'She had to ... to go on a message.' He glanced wildly out of the window. 'I'm afraid you'll have to leave now. I have things to do. I'll see you all next week,' he added, trying very hard to smile naturally.

'That'll be great.' Desmond moved towards the door and they all followed dumbly, shaken by Mr O'Leary's appearance.

No one spoke until they reached the main gate of the harbour.

'There's something very dodgy going on in there!' Brendan exclaimed vehemently as they turned down the road. 'And where's Aisling?'

TWENTY-ONE

'We can't just do nothing!' Brendan insisted. 'There's something far wrong.'

'Very far wrong,' Claire exclaimed. 'And it's not like Aisling just to go off somewhere and not say. Even if she had to go, she would have rung me. She's like that. She hates to let anyone down.'

'Maybe we could ring her mother anyway,' Doyle suggested tentatively.

'No.' Desmond shook his head. 'Mr O'Leary was obviously putting us off ringing. He must have had his reasons.'

'If there is something wrong, he won't want to worry Mrs O'Leary unless it's really necessary,' Claire pointed out. 'She's six months pregnant now, and she hasn't been so well this time.'

'So what are we going to do?' Brendan demanded.

Instinctively they all looked at Desmond — even Claire, who was the brainy one. There was something about Desmond's calm approach to things that always suggested he would know what was best. It had been his idea to cross the river and walk along the south bank as they had planned to. Not that they were very enthusiastic. Doyle had the photocopied map in his hand, but so far they hadn't glanced at it.

Desmond answered honestly. 'I don't know what to

do,' he said. 'But I'm working on it.' He pulled a small pair of binoculars from his pocket. 'I brought these along,' he told them. 'Anyone want a go?'

Brendan glanced at them. 'Smart. Top of the range,' he said, without his usual energy. 'Are they your father's? Won't they be missed?'

'Not if they're back before he is,' Desmond told him; but the words, which normally would have made them all laugh, hardly raised a smile.

Doyle held out his hand. 'Can I have a look?' he asked.

'Sure.'

'Gosh, they're fantastic.' Doyle adjusted the lens. 'I can even read the number-plate on that white van going along Bachelor's Walk. 152 AD. I've seen that number before, somewhere .... It's turned up the lane to Paddy's Cove.'

'A white transit van, was it?' Brendan asked.

'Yes.'

'I bet that's the one I just missed hitting at the far side of the roundabout.' Brendan grimaced. 'On my way to the harbour. You should have seen the look I got. Talk about road rage!' He stopped for a moment, then exclaimed, 'That's who the driver was! I couldn't place him. It was that man we saw with the Liam guy down at the harbour. Remember?'

'I've got it!' Doyle exclaimed. 'Where I saw the number! It was when their van was leaving the harbour. You're right, Brendan. And that guy — Joe — was the one who nicked our film,' he added without thinking, forgetting that he hadn't told any of them about his suspicions.

Desmond stared at him. 'Did you think that too? I thought maybe I was jumping to conclusions.'

'Me too. But what else could have happened to it?'

Doyle said — although he did have some reservations. 'Aisling said her father didn't find it. What's wrong, Claire?' he asked, interrupting himself as she gasped. Her face had gone deathly white.

'That man. The one you're talking about. He was in a car and he stopped to talk to us — to Aisling, really. On Sunday, after we left the café. He sort of made a fuss of Aisling. He asked how the project was going.' Claire bit her lip. 'I tried to sort of ignore him, but you know what Aisling's like. She hates to be rude in case she hurts anyone. What if she's been kidnapped?' she asked, horror-stricken.

'Why would anyone do that?' Brendan demanded.

'It happens,' Claire said.

Doyle realised that they were all looking at Desmond again, looking for leadership of some sort.

At the same moment he remembered that his father had been going to the harbour, to give clearance to a van. But there hadn't been a van in the compound.

'There wasn't a van at the harbour,' he said into the stricken silence.

Desmond held his gaze. 'Should there have been?' he asked steadily.

Doyle nodded. 'In the compound. My father was going there at two o'clock to give it clearance.'

'Or not, maybe,' Desmond said slowly. His eyes gleamed with the steely glint Doyle had noticed when he had spoken to the boy in the café who had started to tease Claire.

Brendan gave a long whistle. 'Drugs! Someone must have been suspicious, for the van to be put in the compound.'

'But why would they take Aisling?' Claire almost whispered the question.

'We don't know that they did,' Desmond cautioned.

He was alert and businesslike now. 'But let's try and put everything we know together. Try and think back. See if there are any other clues.'

This was the other side to Desmond's character, Doyle realised, the side he had only caught a glimpse of now and again. The way he responded to a challenge — determined, weighing up the best approach. That was probably why he was so good at the hurling.

'Was Liam in the van this morning, when you nearly ran into it?' Desmond asked Brendan.

'No.'

'He was at the marina on Sunday,' Doyle said. 'I saw him going onto a yacht.'

Desmond looked at him quickly. 'When was that, then?'

'In the evening.' Doyle returned his gaze. 'When you were on a fishing-boat. I saw you as I passed.'

'A friend of my father's asked him to help with some repairs,' Desmond said. 'I went along.' He frowned suddenly. 'At least, that's what they said. Dave works with Dad, though,' he added thoughtfully.

'Maybe they were on some sort of watch,' Claire interrupted. 'I heard Uncle Frank tell Da that he had to spend today over at the fishing harbour. Desmond's father's in the Gardaí,' she explained, seeing Doyle's puzzled look.

So that's why Desmond doesn't want to talk about what his dad does! Doyle thought. There had been a boy at the school in Brussels whose father was a policeman, and he had hated people knowing. He said nobody at school would tell him anything in case he repeated it and got them into trouble. And everybody expected him to be goody-goody all the time. Doyle had understood how the boy felt. In a way, he was in the same position; even Brendan had taken it for granted that he couldn't be into drugs just because his parents worked for Customs. He wasn't, but it didn't necessarily follow.

'Doyle, didn't you say your parents both had to work today?' Brendan said, interrupting his thoughts.

'Yes. There's been some sort of surveillance going on down at the fishing harbour. It might have to do with that. Not that I'm supposed to know,' he added.

'Tell me about it,' Desmond said. 'I think parents sometimes forget we've got ears! But you said Liam was at the marina, didn't you?'

'So the eejits are looking in the wrong place!' Brendan declared. 'Oh, sorry,' he added quickly; 'relatives excepted. I was talking generally, like — the Gardaí and the Customs ....'

'Maybe they're looking in the wrong place, maybe they're not.' Desmond ignored the criticism. 'We'd better not assume too much.'

'Whatever's going on, all this talking isn't helping Aisling,' Clare interrupted impatiently. 'Can't you think of something, Desmond?'

'We could go and have a Coke in Paddy's Cove,' Desmond suggested mildly. 'You were at the far side of the roundabout, Brendan? When you saw the van, like?'

'Yes. Why?'

'In that case, they wouldn't know you were heading for the harbour. And they didn't see us. They won't be suspicious.'

'Would they take Aisling to Paddy's Cove?' Doyle asked doubtfully.

'The van's there,' Desmond responded. 'And it's the only suggestion I can come up with.'

'Right. Let's get moving,' said Brendan.

'You and Doyle go on with the bikes,' Desmond instructed. 'Claire and I will come in as though we'd all arranged to meet in the café. Keep it casual,' he warned.

Brendan was already well on his way to the bridge
before Doyle had mounted his bicycle. He followed
more cautiously, his heart in his mouth at some of
Brendan's manoeuvres among the traffic. If that was
the way Brendan had been cycling earlier, no wonder
the van driver had shown signs of road rage.

A thought struck him.

Had Aisling been in the van then?

TWENTY-TWO

Brendan slowed down as they approached the café, allowing Doyle to catch up. 'I hope we're on the right track — that Aisling is here somewhere. She must be scared stiff,' he said.

'Ye-es ....' Doyle tried hard to get the niggling doubt out of the back of his mind, but it persisted. And yet, Mr O'Leary had been genuinely upset. No one could have put that on. But then, he might have been having second thoughts, in case he had put Aisling in danger .... And anyway, even if he was in with the smugglers, and the kidnapping had been arranged to cover up his involvement, she wouldn't have known — so she would still be terrified. Surely her father wouldn't willingly put her through that?

And yet, it all seemed too pat. After all, Mr O'Leary *could* have got the Gardaí and let them handle it. They would have known what to do.

Doyle's mind was in turmoil. What if Aisling was in danger — in real danger? He might have been able to prevent that, if he had talked to his father about his suspicions of Liam, about the fact that the café dealt drugs. What made him feel even worse was the realisation that it wasn't just the lack of communication between himself and his father that had made it difficult. For one thing, he hadn't wanted to be given out to for eavesdropping. And then there had been Aisling's father; he hadn't wanted to grass. That was fair enough. But he knew in his heart that his reason for that was selfish. He liked Aisling, of course, and he didn't want her to be hurt; but the real reason had been that he hadn't wanted to lose her friendship or the others'. And he would have — if Mr O'Leary was in on anything.

But after all, I don't know for sure that Aisling's in danger, Doyle thought, excusing himself. He had been jumping to conclusions, simply because Mr O'Leary was so generous. But he was still uneasy.

Brendan looked at him closely as they drew to a halt. 'What's worrying you?' he asked. 'Do you know something the rest of us don't?'

'It's just ....' Doyle took a long breath. 'It's just that I wondered where Mr O'Leary gets all the money,' he blurted out. 'I mean, the job can't be all that well paid, can it?'

Brendan stared at him. 'Surely you didn't think that Mr O'Leary would be in on something like drug-running!'

'It was just that he's so generous and ... and all that.' Doyle knew his face was scarlet. He should have kept his mouth shut. Brendan would probably never speak to him again.

'You eejit!' Brendan started to laugh. 'There's no way Mr O'Leary would risk losing his job. Especially at the rate he's getting through his lottery win.'

'Lottery win?'

'Yes. A good few thousand, as far as I know. And he's like that — generous, like. To a fault, my mam says.'

'I didn't know,' Doyle mumbled. He felt worse than ever. Jumping to the wrong conclusions and thinking himself smart ... it wasn't the first time he had done that. 'I'm sorry,' he said lamely. 'It was a rotten thing to think.'

'Probably,' Brendan said mildly. 'But reasonable enough, when you didn't know the story. I suppose throwing all that money about would be enough to raise suspicions,' he added thoughtfully. 'Just as well Des's father knows about the win.' He shrugged. 'Forget it.'

'You won't ....' Doyle forced himself to look directly at Brendan. 'You won't tell the others, will you?' How was he ever going to face Aisling if she knew what he had thought?

'Not a chance,' Brendan said. 'We're mates, aren't we? Forget it, like I said. Come on, we'll go on in.'

Doyle followed, relieved by Brendan's matter-of-fact acceptance of his mistake — and by the fact that he had been mistaken. He stopped, though, as they approached the door.

'Hold on,' he said. 'The man in the van — Joe. He's bound to recognise us from down at the harbour.'

'Good point.' Brendan bit his lip. 'Let's check round the back and see if the van's there.'

It was. At least, there was a white van parked behind the café. But the number-plate was different; it read clearly, '222 ZZ'.

'It's not the one I saw through the binoculars,' Doyle said.

'Nor the one at the roundabout,' Brendan added. 'You were sure of the number?'

'Positive. Could they have changed the number-plate?'

'Maybe.' Brendan bit his lip. 'And it's a funny-looking number anyway.' He sidled over to the van and peered through the back window. 'There's just two cases in there,' he said. 'The man's luggage, like. He

must be going on somewhere. I hope he's not planning
on taking Aisling! Come on — we might not have
much time. Let's go into the café and see if that Joe is
there. Then we can be sure. We'll have to risk being
recognised. And after all, as far as he knows, we don't
know anything about what's going on. Come to think
of it,' he added, 'we don't know if anything *is* going on!'

When they entered the café there was no sign of Joe,
nor of Liam. The relief assistant whom they had seen
the previous Sunday was at the counter. Voices were
coming from the back room, though. Doyle stopped in
front of the selection of cakes, trying to pick up the
words of the conversation.

'Do you want one?' the assistant asked.

'Not yet, thanks,' Doyle told him. 'We're waiting for
two friends. I'm just looking.'

'Don't spoil your appetite,' the man joked, moving
away to wipe a table as two workmen went out.

Doyle strained his ears. Snatches of the conversation
drifted through to him. One voice was definitely Joe's;
and the other was familiar. It was the man who had
called to Liam from the kitchen, that time they had
been by the outhouse, Doyle realised — the one Liam
had called 'Boss'. But where else had he heard it?

'You shouldn't have brought the van here,' the Boss
declared. 'Not when they're on to you. And where's
Liam gone?'

'The stuff had to be picked up. It's been down there
too long as it is. We don't want accidents. Just as well
to take it with what came off the ferry.' That was the
van driver, Joe.

'Can you shift it, now the heat's gone?' the Boss
asked. 'Are there still takers?'

'Sure. The gang I deal with will take anything that's
going. They'll know where to shift it. It's just as well to

take it with the dope that came off the ferry,' Joe told him. 'Liam agreed back on Sunday,' he added. 'The yacht leaves at two today. There's no problem. The authorities have had their eyes glued to the fishing harbour for the past ten days. You know yourself there's been no sign of them at the marina.'

Of course! thought Doyle, remembering where else he had heard the Boss's voice. The man at the marina — the one varnishing the boat. He must have been keeping watch.

'And Liam's gone to get his gear. The guy at the harbour would recognise him, so he's coming out with me. You'll have to find yourself another assistant.' That was Joe again.

'And the girl? That was madness.'

Doyle's heart was pounding so hard he could hardly hear for the drumming in his ears. He looked quickly to make sure the assistant wasn't watching and leaned forward slightly.

'Don't panic,' Joe said. 'We'll shift her — take her in the van and leave it somewhere before the yacht sails. She doesn't know where she is, and she never saw you. There's no problem. The van will be found, even with the fake number-plates. She'll do exactly as she's told.'

'Have you come to a decision?'

Doyle jumped. The assistant was watching him with amusement.

'You're practically drooling over them,' he said.

'Here's the others,' Doyle answered, forcing a grin. 'I'll have to consult them.'

'And no doubt you'll require a knife,' the man said, with a laugh and a glance at Claire as she and Desmond joined Brendan at the window table.

'Probably.' Doyle forced himself to laugh back as he moved away.

'What have you been doing over there?' Brendan hissed at him.

'Listening to a conversation between that Joe and the guy who was in the kitchen — the Boss,' Doyle told them in a low voice. He looked at Desmond. 'I saw the Boss down at the marina. I think he was watching the gardaí watching the fishing-boats.'

'Typical,' Brendan murmured.

'But what about Aisling?' Claire demanded. 'Did they say anything?'

'Yes. They've definitely got her.'

'Where?'

'I don't know,' Doyle answered miserably. 'They didn't say.'

TWENTY-THREE

'Have you got the map?' Desmond asked Doyle.

'Yes. Here it is.' Doyle took the map out of his pocket and laid it on the table. 'What do you want it for?'

Desmond spread it out. 'So that it looks like we're discussing this.' He put his finger on a point at random and, with his eyes intent on the map, asked, 'What exactly did they say about Aisling?'

Doyle tried to think clearly. 'Joe did say that they'd leave her in the van for the guards to find.'

'Is she in the van now?'

'No. Brendan checked it. It's out the back. They said they would take her in it. I sort of got the impression she might be around here, though. Maybe we should call the Gardaí.'

Desmond shook his head. 'That might put her in real danger. Probably Mr O'Leary was told to keep quiet — or else. At least we know they do mean her to be found.'

'But if the Customs people go to the harbour, they're going to find out anyway,' Claire declared. 'They won't do nothing. Will they?' she asked, looking at Doyle.

'They would know the best thing to do, I suppose,' Doyle said. 'They're not going till two o'clock, though — and the yacht sails at two!' he exclaimed.

'Keep your voice down — and your eyes,' Desmond cautioned. 'What yacht?'

'The one I saw Liam going onto on Sunday, I suppose,' Doyle explained. 'Joe said they had arranged to pick up "the stuff" — whatever that is — and take it to the yacht in the van, with whatever it is they brought over in the ferry. That's when they said about Aisling.'

Claire gave a sigh of relief. 'She should be all right, then. And we can tell the guards at two.'

'We'd need to be sure first,' Desmond pointed out.

'But they'll get clear with the drugs — and they'll get away with kidnapping her!' Brendan hissed indignantly. 'And that's two hours yet. We don't know what they've done to her!'

Doyle interrupted them quietly. 'I think we'd better buy something,' he said. 'The man at the counter is giving us funny looks.' He took his money out of his pocket. 'How much have we got?'

The others produced their money, and Doyle counted the total. 'Should be enough for four Cokes and two buns,' he said.

'You'd better get them,' Brendan said, 'since the man thinks you spent all that time choosing which to have. I'm going to the Gents. I won't be a minute.'

'I'll just take these coffees through to the Boss,' the assistant told Doyle as he approached. 'Then I'll get your order.'

There was a murmur of voices, and the noise of cutlery against dishes, from the back room. They must be having a meal, Doyle decided.

The assistant returned, closing the communicating door behind him, and Doyle gave his order.

'Here you are,' the assistant said. 'That'll be four pound eighty.'

'Thanks.' Doyle glanced at Brendan, on his way back from the toilet. His face was flushed and his eyes bright. He looked as though he was bursting with information.

Surely they hadn't locked Aisling in the men's toilets!

'What's happened?' Doyle asked, as Desmond folded the map and made room for the tray on the table.

Brendan was talking to Claire in a low voice, but his excitement was obvious.

'That CD you were telling Aisling was old hat — you know, the one with the scratches, the one that keeps skipping lines — has she still got it?' he asked.

'The Spice Girls one?'

'Yeah.'

'I think so.'

'She has,' Doyle told them, as he sat down. 'She asked me yesterday to fix the strap on the carrying-case for the personal CD player her father gave her. She had it then.' He felt himself flush and avoided looking at Brendan. At the time, although he had wondered at the expensive present given for no apparent reason, he had been flattered. Afterwards, he had thought that maybe Aisling hadn't really needed his help — that it had been a sort of excuse to be with him. That had been flattering too.

'Why do you want to know?' he asked.

'Because right now what she really, really wants is to get out of wherever she is!'

'Where?' Claire gasped.

'In the Gents?' Desmond frowned.

Brendan took a sip of his Coke and shot a quick look in the direction of the counter, but the assistant was busy and had his back to them.

'No. But the music is coming up through the ... the drains,' he said.

Claire stared at him. 'They haven't put her down in the sewer, have they?'

'I wouldn't think so,' Desmond said. 'But she must be somewhere under the building!'

'How would she manage to play it that loud?' Doyle asked doubtfully. 'She only had earphones.'

'The sound must be echoing through the drains,' Desmond explained. 'It's probably not all that loud.'

Brendan let his breath out between his teeth. 'I bet she's where they've got the drugs stashed! Down that drain in the outhouse, like I thought!'

He half-rose from his seat, but Desmond stopped him.

'Take it easy,' he said. 'We can't go rushing out.' He looked at Doyle. 'Did you see the men just now?'

'No, but I heard their voices. Sounded like they were having a meal.'

'We can't leave her there,' Claire put in desperately. 'She'll be terrified — and if we get her out, then we can tell the guards and they'll catch the men.'

'It might not be that easy,' Desmond warned her, finishing his half-bun and taking a gulp of Coke.

'We can try,' Brendan insisted.

'Too true, we can. We're not going to leave her there if we can help it,' Desmond told him. 'But rushing out is only going to look suspicious.' He thought for a moment, then said, 'Brendan, you and Doyle go out normally and collect your bikes as though you were leaving. Park them round the back, somewhere out of sight. Claire and I will walk up the lane and then double back. You two leave first.'

'OK.' Brendan turned to Doyle. 'Coming?'

'Yes. See you later,' Doyle said as he left the table. As they passed the counter he called, 'Thanks. See you.'

'See you,' the assistant responded, lifting his head from a newspaper.

'Not too soon, I hope,' Brendan murmured in Doyle's ear. 'And I hope that Liam isn't round at the van!'

He wasn't. The back yard was still deserted, the van still parked in the same place. Doyle gave a nervous glance towards the back window of the building, but realised that anyone inside would have to stand up and look out in order to see them.

Desmond and Claire arrived as Brendan was turning the key in the outhouse door.

'They must be pretty sure of themselves, leaving this in the door,' he remarked, slipping inside.

Desmond took the key out and put it in his pocket as he pulled the door closed behind them. 'Just in case we get locked in,' he said calmly. In the dim light from the one small window, he looked at the iron cover in the centre of the concrete floor. 'I hope we'll be able to lift that,' he said.

'This will be what they use.' Brendan reached for a crowbar propped in a corner. He slid it into a notch at the edge of the cover and pressed down. Nothing happened. 'Give me a hand,' he gasped, his face red with exertion.

With Doyle and Claire helping, the cover gradually lifted until Desmond was able to grasp the underside and slide it onto the floor. Breathless, they stared down into the darkness, listening for the unmistakable strains of 'Wannabe'.

TWENTY-FOUR

'It's pitch-black,' Claire declared, as they stared down into total silence. 'We won't be able to see a thing! And where is she? There's not a sound.'

Desmond looked at Brendan. 'Are you positive about the music?' he asked.

'Positive. She must have switched it off,' Brendan said. 'We've got Doyle's torch,' he added.

'Where did that come from?' Desmond asked, as Doyle produced a slim pencil-like torch from his pocket.

'It came with the bike,' Doyle told him. 'In the tool-bag. It's got a great beam.'

He flashed it downwards and moved the beam from side to side. There was a drop of perhaps six feet, into what looked like a large concrete pipe about three feet across. They could hear the sound of running water, but there was no sign of anything flowing through the actual drain.

'It's bone-dry,' Brendan exclaimed, with a glance at Claire. 'Definitely not a sewer. What are we waiting for?'

'We don't all need to go,' Desmond told him.

'Yes, we do.' Brendan dropped down into the hole and looked up. 'Come on,' he urged.

Desmond shrugged, then looked at Claire. 'Claire, you —' he began.

'No way!' she exclaimed. 'I'm not waiting here on my own!'

'We'd better make it quick, then,' Desmond told her. 'You go next.'

Doyle followed Claire, with Desmond bringing up the rear.

'This way.' Brendan pointed to his left. 'Here, Doyle, give me the torch.' He shone the beam to the right. 'It's blocked off there,' he said. 'The water seems to be running in another pipe alongside.'

'It must have been diverted for some reason,' Desmond said, as the light from the torch played over the area.

Brendan gave a whistle. 'Look,' he exclaimed. 'Fish-boxes!' He shone the beam directly onto the side of one. 'HADDOCK,' large black letters declared. 'First time I've seen a box of fish that didn't stink.' He crawled towards the box. Handing the torch to Desmond, he lifted the lid and sniffed. 'Funny-looking haddock!'

Desmond shuffled over to him, then grabbed Brendan's arm as he reached out to prod individually wrapped bundles of a greyish-white substance. 'Don't,' he warned urgently. 'It might be unstable!'

'*Unstable*?' Brendan gaped at him. 'You mean it's not heroin — or anything like that?'

'No. It's Semtex. You see it on TV sometimes. And I've seen pictures of it in Da's journals.'

Doyle felt the blood drain from his face. No wonder Liam had got so steamed up, that time Brendan had been about to light a cigarette. And this was what Joe and the Boss had meant when they talked about 'it' having been here for too long, and about not wanting an accident. It must have been here since before the Good Friday peace agreement, he realised. Joe must be planning to sell it to some splinter group that's out to wreck the agreement — like the ones who planted that bomb in Omagh last year ....

And they had put Aisling down here with it!

'Where's Aisling?' he hissed. The sooner they were all out of there, the better.

'Let's find her and get clear.' There was just the hint of a tremor in Brendan's voice as he replaced the lid of the box. 'She must be in the other direction.'

More shaken than any of them would admit, they crouched low, half-crawling through the pipe in single file, away from the explosives. After a few feet, the concrete sides disappeared and the opening narrowed slightly. The beam of the torch picked out the reddish brown of rusting metal all around them.

Doyle heard Claire's sharp intake of breath at the same moment as the realisation dawned on him. Jock's old oil drums! The weakness must have been discovered sometime since Jock had worked there, and, just as Desmond had suggested, the flow of water had been diverted. This was where Jock had found the axe-head — where the coins might be!

In the dimness he saw Claire reach out a hand towards the disintegrating metal, as though somehow she might sense the tragedy her father had described.

A shiver ran down Doyle's spine. There would be bones here, too, the remains of those hundred Highlanders who had perished. And there would be other weapons besides the explosives — broadswords, Lochaber axes .... Less lethal than the Semtex, Doyle thought; and at least they would have been used in one-to-one fighting, not like the Semtex which had caused so much destruction in Ireland over the past decades. And Miss Binchly had talked about the civilising effects of the past millennium! That was a laugh!

Desmond was calling Aisling's name in a low voice

and flashing the torch. There was no response.

Ahead, the oil-drum walls gave way to concrete piping again. Jock's Gaffer couldn't have used many of the drums, Doyle realised; he must have simply sandwiched a few between sections of concrete piping.

'There she is!' Claire exclaimed suddenly. 'Aisling!' she called out urgently.

There was no answer.

TWENTY-FIVE

Aisling was huddled against the cold concrete of the pipe, turned slightly away from them, her body twitching.

Desmond hesitated; then, with a glance at the others' apprehensive faces, he shone the torch onto her face. Her eyes, which had been closed, opened immediately, and she sat up with a start. Dazzled, she took a moment or two to recognise them. In the same moments, Doyle heard the buzzing of sound from her CD player and realised that she had the earphones in her ears. No wonder she hadn't heard them calling! And her twitching had been keeping time to the song. He almost laughed out loud with relief. Beside her lay an open box containing two small red speakers, obviously newly bought. She must have been trying them out earlier.

Claire was kneeling beside her. 'Aisling, are you all right?' she asked, grasping Aisling's hand.

The blue eyes filled with tears. 'Oh, Claire,' was all Aisling could say at first. Then, swallowing hard, she gave a watery smile. 'I'm fine. Just cold. The man took my fleece — to prove to Da that he had me. I moved along here because it didn't seem quite so dark, but there's cold air coming from somewhere, I think.'

She straightened and looked around at the others.

'Where have you come from? How did you find me? Did you go to the harbour?' she asked urgently. 'Is Da all right? They didn't hurt him, did they?'

'No. Not that way,' Claire hastened to reassure her. 'But he's dead worried about you. What happened?' Then, as her hand brushed against Aisling's bare arm, she exclaimed, 'You're frozen!'

Doyle had his fleece off before anyone could move. 'Here,' he told Aisling. 'Put this on.'

'But what about you?' she asked, hugging its warmth to her chest.

'We're not staying long,' Doyle replied with a grin. He added seriously, with a glance at Desmond, 'Actually, we'll need to hurry.'

'I can't,' Aisling said.

They all stared at her. 'What do you mean, you can't?' Brendan demanded.

'The man said if I didn't stay and do what he said, they would hurt Da.'

'The rotten pig!' Brendan exploded. 'Is that why you came here with him? Were you at the harbour, like?'

Aisling shook her head. 'No. I went into town early to buy speakers. The man stopped in his car and asked if I was going to the harbour. He said he was going to see Da, and did I want a lift.'

'You got into his car!' Claire shook her head in disbelief. 'After all we've been told about taking lifts from strangers?'

'Well, I didn't think he was a stranger — not really,' Aisling pointed out. 'We saw him at the harbour with Da. And he talked to us one day, remember?'

'So how did you get here?' Desmond asked.

'Where's here?'

'Below Paddy's Cove.'

'I thought so! I heard that door squeak. I remembered

it doing that when Brendan opened it, that time we were looking for the coins,' she exclaimed triumphantly.

'Couldn't you see?' Doyle asked.

'No. He put a scarf or something over my eyes.'

'But didn't you struggle or anything? Weren't you scared?'

'Yes, but there was no way I wanted Da to get hurt, so I just did what the man said.'

Doyle looked at her with open admiration. There had been no heroics in her voice; her words were just a statement of fact, based on the way she felt about her father. For her it was as simple as that.

'I didn't think about him being so worried, though,' she added naïvely. 'I thought the man would tell him that I wouldn't be hurt — they were only keeping me so he'd let them have the van, like — and that would make it all right.' Her eyes widened suddenly. 'You don't think Da would have rung Mam, would he?' she asked, looking at Claire. 'The doctor said she wasn't to get too stressed or she might lose the baby!'

Desmond answered quickly. 'No. He didn't. And he made an excuse when we asked if we could ring and see if you were at home — he said you'd gone on a message. But if you're missing much longer, your mother will have to be told. That's why you have to come with us,' he urged. 'And your da will be OK. As soon as we get clear, we can contact the guards — and I'll ring my father to go straight down to the harbour. Come on, put Doyle's fleece on and we'll get moving.'

Aisling frowned. 'If Da didn't tell you what had happened, how did you know?' she asked, puzzled.

'Desmond's detective work,' Brendan joked. 'No matter how hard he tries, he just can't get away from the fact that his da's a garda! That and the fact that I heard the Spice Girls yelling their heads off in the

Gents in Paddy's Cove. Come on, though; we've got to hurry. Everything will be all right. Don't worry.'

Aisling looked at Desmond as she pulled on Doyle's fleece. 'Will Da not get hurt?'

'No,' he reassured her.

'OK, I'll come.'

'Let's go, then.' Brendan twisted round and edged back along the drain.

The others followed, one behind the other. Claire hesitated at the point where the concrete piping gave way to the rusting oil drums, but Desmond hurried her on.

'There could be something here — something else like the axe-head,' she said.

'Maybe. But we haven't time to look,' Desmond told her sharply. 'And anyway, it'd be dangerous to disturb the sides. The whole lot could cave in and bury us! Come on — we need every minute.'

Brendan was already standing below the opening which led back into the outhouse. 'Who's going first?' he asked.

'You go,' Desmond decided. 'Then you can help the others through. You'll have to stand on my back to reach the edge, though. Will you be able to pull yourself through?'

'No problem. But what about the last one up?'

'I'll come last. I'm tallest. Check the yard, though, as soon as you're up. Make sure the coast's clear.'

'Will do.' But Brendan looked dubious as Desmond, on his hands and knees, braced his back. 'Are you sure about this? I'm no lightweight.'

'Get on with it!' Desmond retorted. 'Before I change my mind. Grab the edge as quick as you can, and that'll take some of the weight off me.'

Brendan stepped gingerly onto Desmond's back, reaching upwards at the same time. He grasped the edge of the opening and, strong arms heaving, lifted himself into the outhouse.

'Great.' Desmond gave a grunt of satisfaction. 'Check the yard.'

They waited, listening, as the door squeaked open. Then there was silence, followed by the quick scuffle of Brendan's feet.

'All clear,' he announced, grinning down at them. 'Aisling next, is it?'

'It is.' Desmond made the decision, and no one disagreed. 'Up you go, Aisling.'

As Aisling balanced on Desmond's back and stretched up to grab the edge of the opening, Brendan reached down towards her. Grasping her under the armpits, he half-lifted, half-pulled her upwards. In moments, she was sitting on the outhouse floor beside him. Claire followed, then Doyle.

'Keep a watch at the door,' Desmond warned. He stood on tiptoe, his fingers just able to grasp the edge of the hole. With a grunt, he lifted his feet off the ground and pulled his elbows to waist level. Slowly his head appeared in the opening. Brendan leant forward to hoist him up and over — just as his fingers slipped. They heard the swear-word and the dull thud almost in the same moment.

Claire leaned over in alarm. 'Are you all right?' she called.

'Yes, I think so. Brendan,' Desmond said, 'you'd better grab my wrists as soon as I've got a hold.'

'Hang on,' Brendan told him. 'There's an empty box here. I'll pass it down to you. That'll make it easier.'

'Is someone watching the door?' Desmond demanded, as he reached for the box.

'Claire is now,' Doyle put in. 'Can you manage?'

'Fine.' Desmond had his elbows on the floor of the

outhouse, and in seconds he was standing beside the others. 'OK,' he instructed. 'Let's get out of here.'

Claire swung the door open, and they crowded into the yard.

The sound of men's voices reached them from the side of the café.

'Right. Scarper!' Desmond hissed.

Too late.

Liam, followed by Joe and the Boss, rounded the corner.

An oath exploded from Liam. 'It's those Y2Kids!' he spat.

'Stay where you are!' Joe rapped out, reaching into his pocket. 'Don't move. I've a gun — and I'll use it if I have to!'

TWENTY-SIX

'Back inside!' Desmond spat out the words as the man fumbled in an inside pocket.

They moved as one, turning, pushing through the door of the outhouse, Desmond's broad frame guarding the rear. Brendan had a hand to the door as Desmond swung in behind them. Doyle was with him immediately, helping to bang it closed and throwing his weight against it as Desmond, with calm precision, inserted the key. A quick turn in the lock and he stood back, looking at the others grimly.

'What about the gun?' Claire asked, her face white and her fingers nervously easing the legs of her spectacles.

'He won't use it. The shot would attract attention,' Desmond told her. 'But shh — listen.'

Doyle felt goose-pimples rise on his skin as they stood, ears cocked to hear what was happening beyond the door. The door-handle turned, slowly at first, then rattled as whoever had his hand on it realised the door was locked. There was a string of swear-words, followed by a shudder as someone slammed his shoulder against the door. The thick wood held firm.

'Liam!' It was the Boss's voice. 'Get the spare key — and make it snappy!'

'That's torn it!' Brendan exclaimed. 'What now, Des?'

'We'll have to go back down the pipe and try and

hide somewhere,' Desmond decided. 'They'll have to
get the key out of this side before they can open the
door. That'll give us breathing space.' He glanced at his
watch. 'You said the yacht was due to leave at two
o'clock, was it?' he asked, glancing at Doyle.

'That's what they said. To catch the tide, I think.'

'They'll need all their time, then. If we go along the
drain, they won't want to risk delaying the departure
by chasing us. Chances are, they'll grab the stuff and
make a run for it. They'll probably lock us in, but we'll
have to chance it.'

Doyle nodded in agreement. Des was always so
cool; he seemed to think of everything, as though he
could anticipate the men's every move. Perhaps he
read a lot of detective novels — or maybe he picked up
hints from his father's Garda journals. If anyone could
get them out of this, Des could.

They dropped back down through the opening, one
after the other: Brendan first, then the girls, then Doyle.
By the time Desmond joined them, the others were
well inside the drain, crouched beyond the rusting oil
drums, in the section of concrete piping where Aisling
had been.

Behind them they heard the sound of the key falling
to the floor, then the turn of the spare one in the lock.
The door squeaked open, and the men swore as they
found the outhouse empty.

There was a scuffling in the outhouse, then a thud.
Doyle held his breath and pressed his hands against
the piping to keep them from trembling. Liam had
jumped down into the drain. He was only a few yards
away.

A torch illuminated the opening of the drain.

'They're not there,' said Liam's voice. 'They've
made off along the pipe. Here, you kids!' he yelled.

'Come out of there or we'll blast you out!'

Desmond signalled with his hand, urging the others backwards. They shuffled along as silently as they could.

The beam of Liam's torch swept along the line of the pipe, penetrating the darkness.

'There they are!' he shouted triumphantly.

'Let them be,' Joe told him sharply, from above. 'There's no time to waste. You and the Boss get the stuff up while I reverse the van to the door. We'll be well away before they get out of here. I'll make sure of that,' he added grimly. 'Just tell them to keep their distance and no one will get hurt.'

'Hear that?' Liam shouted, as the light swung away from them and Joe joined him in the pipe. 'Stay where you are!'

As though we'd do anything else, Doyle thought, shifting a leg from under him. They could hear the men cursing and swearing as the boxes were eased out of the drain. God help us if any of that stuff goes off, he thought with a shiver. If it's been there a long time, it could be unstable .... He felt rather than saw Desmond's quick glance in his direction; no doubt he was having the same thoughts.

They huddled close together, waiting in the darkened silence to find out what the men would do once all the boxes had been taken up.

They heard the purr of the van's engine in the yard — faint at first, then clearer as it was revved up. It came again; then they heard someone cursing. The engine stopped, and a door banged. A voice called down to Liam, and he shouted back.

Desmond edged forward, his head cocked sideways, listening. Doyle followed, peering towards the opening.

Liam had gone up a short ladder which had been

lowered into the drain. There was no sign of the Boss.
Two boxes lay at the bottom of the ladder.

Desmond signalled to the others not to come any
closer. Squatting there, he and Doyle listened to what
was happening above.

They heard the van's engine restart, then the sound
of the wheels turning on gravel — then skidding. The
engine stopped; started again; more skidding. The
engine stopped once more, and the van door slammed.

'What's happening?' Doyle hissed.

'Keep quiet,' Desmond warned, as the Boss spoke.

'Didn't you fill in that pothole with more gravel,
Liam?' he demanded roughly. 'I told you about it
yesterday.'

'What's the problem?' Joe asked.

'Some sort of subsidence, apparently,' the Boss told
him. 'There's a dip there, and last night's rain hasn't
helped. Give it another try. I'll give Liam a hand getting
the last of the boxes out of the drain, and then we'll
come and give you a push.'

'What about those kids?' That was Liam.

'We'll use the lock on the drain cover.'

'They might suffocate,' Liam pointed out.

'Serve them right for meddling,' the Boss replied
briskly. 'Come on, now. There's no time to waste.'

Doyle heard Desmond swear under his breath. He
obviously hadn't expected them to close the cover —
and with it locked, there was no way they could get
out on their own. How long would it be before they
were found? If only I'd talked to Dad about the café
and the drug-dealing, Doyle thought. At least it would
have given the guards a lead.

Desmond nudged him, and they moved back to the
others. Above them, they could hear the wheels of the
van skidding again.

'What's wrong with the van?' Brendan asked in a low voice.

'There's some sort of subsidence in the yard. It's got stuck in a pothole.'

'We're off!' Liam shouted along the pipe. 'Make yourselves comfortable!'

'Leave the cover off!' Desmond shouted back.

They waited hopefully as the sound of low voices drifted to them. Then they heard the scrape of the ladder being pulled up, followed by the clang of the heavy iron cover being pushed into place. Had Liam locked it?

'How long will we give them before we try to get out, Des?' Brendan asked. 'If they left that box I handed down, we should be able to shift the cover.'

Desmond glanced quickly at Doyle, but said nothing about the lock the man had mentioned. Above them, they heard the rumble of the van and the urgent revving of the engine.

'Better wait till the van's gone,' Desmond said quietly. 'They probably haven't loaded it up yet.'

He switched on the torch as he spoke, and Claire gave a gasp. 'There's stones falling!' she exclaimed.

Desmond played the light of the torch on the area immediately in front of them. A fine curtain of loose earth and small stones caught at the beam.

'Get back,' he urged. 'Quick! Right back into the concrete piping.'

'The oil drums!' Brendan exclaimed. 'The van's put too much pressure on them. Des, will they hold?'

'Doesn't look like it,' Desmond answered grimly, pushing them further into the pipe. 'But, please God, the concrete will.' In the light from the torch, Doyle saw his face turn white. What if it didn't?

Aisling gave a moan. 'We could be buried alive,' she whispered.

Like the Highlanders, Doyle thought wildly. If our bodies have to be dug out, will their remains be found too?

The curtain of earth and small rubble changed to a cascade of fair-sized rocks. They pushed further back into the pipe and watched, almost mesmerised, as the roof of the drain collapsed.

After what seemed like an eternity, the rumbling stopped.

Doyle wiped dirt from his face and peered into the dust-laden shaft of light as Desmond explored the landslip with the beam of the torch. The section of piping where they cowered was completely blocked off from the exit into the outhouse.

They were entombed.

TWENTY-SEVEN

Doyle looked at the others in the light from the torch. 'What will the men think?' he asked.

'That we've all been buried.' Brendan edged towards the rubble on all fours. 'That we're under there. They'll certainly be in a hurry to leave now!'

'They'll think Da told you to come!' Aisling exclaimed suddenly. 'I never thought.' She gave a half-sob, half-moan. 'They'll go to the harbour and get him.'

'They won't have time,' Doyle tried to reassure her. 'It's nearly one o'clock. They have to get that stuff onto a yacht at the marina before two. It sails then — I heard them say so.'

'And they'll be busy trying to get the van out of that pothole — it must be a lot bigger now!' Desmond put in. 'More than likely, it'll be a while before they even look in the outhouse.' He glanced at Brendan. 'They might not even realise what's happened.'

'All the same, we've got to tell the guards,' Aisling insisted. She looked at Desmond accusingly. 'You said it would be all right!'

Doyle tried again to calm her. 'It will be. The Customs people are going to the harbour at two. They'll tell the guards, and they'll come and look for us. For you,' he added, suddenly realising that nobody knew where the rest of them were.

'You're sure?'

'Yes.'

'You look cold,' Aisling said suddenly. 'Do you want your fleece back? I can still feel that draught.'

'No, I'm fine. But I feel it too.' Doyle looked around, then met Desmond's gaze. 'Des,' he said, 'are you thinking what I am? Put out the torch a minute.'

'Could be,' Desmond said, plunging them into darkness.

Not total darkness. As Aisling had said earlier, it seemed less dark there. Doyle peered along the pipe. Was it his imagination, or could he make out just the suggestion of daylight?

'What do you think, Des?' he asked hopefully.

Desmond switched on the torch and beamed at them. 'Good for you, Aisling,' he said. 'You're more observant than any of us.'

'What are you two on about?' Claire demanded.

'I've got it!' Brendan crowed, from where he was examining the rubble. 'The pipe's open at the other end! It was never closed.'

'Maybe. We might as well carry on through, anyway. We're not going to get out this way, that's for sure,' Desmond told him. 'And don't poke at the rubble, Brendan. We don't want the van on top of us.'

'There's something brown and hard here,' Brendan told him. 'But it's quite loose. It won't do any harm to move it.'

'It'll be just a piece of rusty metal off an oil drum,' Desmond answered impatiently. 'Come on.'

Claire had edged over to Brendan. 'It's not metal,' she said breathlessly. 'Wait, Desmond. It might be important. Shine the torch over here.'

Brendan was easing something out from beneath the pile of earth and stones. As Desmond shone the torch

Y2Kids

in their direction, it slid free.

'What is it?' Doyle asked.

'Hold on.' Brendan pulled off his denim jacket and used it to wipe away loose earth.

Claire put out her hand and touched the object, then ran her fingers over it. Doyle peered over her shoulder. It was round, obviously hard, and appeared to have some kind of knobs on the surface.

Claire's face was alight.

'It's a targe!' she exclaimed triumphantly. 'A sort of shield, like. See, it's made of leather — I think they boiled the hides or something to make them hard ....' Her eyes filled with tears. 'I knew Da was right! What Jock told us — and now this — will prove it.'

Brendan glanced at Desmond. 'There could be more,' he said.

'Maybe, but we're not stopping to look,' Desmond said grimly, as fine earth drifted down from above. He looked at Claire. 'The authorities will have enough to order an archaeological dig,' he told her. 'We've got to get out of here.'

'I know,' she agreed quietly. 'We're coming.'

Doyle saw the strain on Desmond's face. He knew that if anything happened to any of them, Des would blame himself. And they were all, except perhaps Aisling, only too aware of the boxes which were probably still in the outhouse ....

As they began to crawl through the pipe, Aisling suddenly stopped. 'My speakers!' she exclaimed. 'I forgot to put them in the bag with the CD player.'

'I'll get them,' Brendan said from behind her. Handing the targe to Claire, he squirmed a few lengths backwards. 'OK, Aisling, I've got them,' he told her. 'And something else!' he exclaimed suddenly.

'What?' she asked.

'I'll show you later.'

Doyle glanced back. In the shadows thrown by the torch, he caught the suppressed excitement on Brendan's face and saw him push something into his jeans pocket. Brendan caught his glance and, grinning with delight, gave a thumbs-up sign.

Before Doyle could form a question, Desmond had given a shout of relief. In the distance ahead, a disk of daylight was just perceptible.

Dirty and dishevelled, they scrambled after him. The darkness thinned, and a cold shaft of air blew over them. Doyle shivered and was suddenly conscious of the damp feel to his knees. Does the tide bring the river right into the pipe? he wondered. Or is the dampness just from spray blown in by the wind? When is high tide?

His fears were unfounded. As they reached the opening, it became obvious that they were well above the level of the water — and well below the safety of the road above. The mouth of the pipe was flush with a stone embankment. Below them lay the cold greyness of the Liffey. Above them, the walls rose perpendicular — insurmountable.

How were they to get out?

TWENTY-EIGHT

'We're below that bit of the quays that the workmen are digging up. I can hear the machines,' Claire told the others, as she peered out of the opening. 'But how are we going to get up there?' she added in dismay.

'Don't worry,' Brendan joked. 'If that stuff in the outhouse goes up, we'll be out of here like cannon-balls!'

'That's sick. It's no laughing matter,' Desmond retorted. 'If it's still in the outhouse, it's just possible it might. We don't know how bad the rock-fall was. It could set the lot off!'

Aisling glanced at them with a puzzled look. She flushed slightly, then asked outright: 'I thought you said it was hash, Brendan? That doesn't explode, does it?'

'It's not hash,' Brendan told her quietly. 'It's Semtex.'

Aisling stared at him, every muscle in her face working. Doyle thought for a moment that she was going to have hysterics. Then he realised in amazement that she was raging. Her blue eyes were flashing and her mouth set hard.

'*Semtex!*' she exploded. 'You mean those men forced Da to help them collect something like *that* — probably to sell to some kind of psychos? After what happened to my cousin Pat! Da even saw him get blown up! Poor Da — he'll be shattered. I'd like to ... to ....' She stopped, at a loss for words and breath.

'Wouldn't we all,' Brendan said. 'Getting Ireland for the Irish is one thing, but blowing up innocent people is something else — specially since the Good Friday agreement.'

'At any time,' Desmond murmured.

Aisling looked at Brendan. 'The guards have to catch them,' she declared in a determined voice.

'No chance — unless we get out of this hole quickly,' Brendan told her. 'It's after one o'clock. They'll be gone at two.'

'Then we have to get out quickly!' she insisted. 'We can't just wait until someone sees us.'

'How? There isn't even anyone standing across the river who might spot us. And with the racket that pneumatic drill above is making, no one's going to hear us, no matter how loud we shout,' Brendan said pessimistically.

'They'd see someone if she was out there in the river,' Aisling told him quietly.

Doyle stared at her, horrified. But Claire seemed to know what she meant.

'Don't be daft, Aisling,' she exclaimed. 'It's one thing playing a victim for life-saving class in the pool, and another shamming something like that out there! Just look how strong the current is, after all that rain last night. And the water's *disgusting*. And what if nobody saw you?'

Desmond stuck his head out and looked down the river. 'I could swim to the bridge,' he said.

'I doubt it,' Aisling told him. 'It's cold out there. You mightn't make it. I'm not school swimming champion for nothing,' she added, without a hint of boasting. 'And I go swimming in the sea with Da and the boys quite often. Da says I can stand up to the cold far better than the boys.' She looked around at the others. 'I'm going to try the drowning bit first, though, before I try swimming to somewhere where I can climb up. It'll be quicker.'

Brendan stared down into the wind-whipped wavelets. 'How do you plan to get into the water?' he asked. 'You can't stand up and dive.'

'I can manage a sitting dive, I think.'

'You *think*!' Doyle couldn't believe his ears. 'Aisling, it's too risky. Des, you can't let her do it!' he cried. This was an Aisling he hadn't known existed.

'He can't stop me,' Aisling told him. 'It'll be OK, Doyle. I know what I'm doing — and Des knows well I can do it.'

'I'm not that confident,' Desmond muttered, as she pulled off the fleece.

'Here, Doyle,' she said. 'Here's your fleece back. And look after my CD player for me,' she added, handing it to him and starting to undo her shoes.

Doyle swallowed. 'Are you sure you can do it?'

'Yes. I'm not quite as timid as Old Jock thought,' she said with a grin. 'I just don't like seeing people the worse for drink.' She laughed at Doyle's expression. 'Claire told me what he said.'

'Push yourself off the wall with your feet,' Desmond advised as they edged back to allow Aisling to sit, shoulders hunched, head down and feet dangling over the edge of the opening. 'And tell the first person you see to call the Gardaí.'

'You bet,' she said. And, after only a moment's hesitation, she was gone.

Doyle clung to the fleece, his heart racing. What if she didn't make it? What if she had misjudged and hit the wall? He could feel the warmth of her body still in the fleece and smell the faint perfume of the soap she used. He hardly dared to look down into the river.

A heartfelt sigh from Desmond reassured him: Aisling had made it. He edged forward and looked down. She was striking out, away from the wall, into the river. It looked cold and unwelcoming. Beside him the others watched, tense and silent. They saw her look up towards the wall which ran along the quay, then swim on. Again she looked up, as though making sure that she could be seen.

Above them, the noise from the pneumatic drill suddenly stopped. At the same moment Aisling began to call out, thrashing about in the water.

Desmond reacted quickly. 'Right, everyone,' he instructed grimly, 'give it all you've got.' And, taking a deep breath, he began to shout for all he was worth.

Below them, Aisling went under once, twice ....

'Des,' Doyle declared, tearing off his trainers, 'I'm going in!'

TWENTY-NINE

.

'Wait!' Claire caught Doyle's arm. 'She's shamming.'

Above them, a man's voice was calling for a lifebelt. 'Holy Mary, help her!' they heard him say. 'Why didn't I learn to swim?'

Minutes later, his prayers turned to swearing as Aisling struck out strongly with sure strokes. 'Why couldn't she have done that in the first place,' he demanded of someone, 'instead of giving us all near-heart-attacks?'

'Wow, isn't she a marvel!' Brendan whooped in delight. 'No wonder she won the championship.'

Aisling had reached the lifebelt. She was letting herself be pulled towards the wall, and shouting to the man to call the Gardaí before he pulled her up.

'Best have you up first,' he shouted down.

She shook her head. 'No, ring them!'

The man spoke to someone behind him. 'Right, then,' he called. 'My mate's doing it. Keep your feet against the wall and a tight hold on the rope.'

Aisling waved to the others as she was hauled up, and Brendan gave way to nervous laughter. 'Would you look at her!' he gasped. 'If Old Jock was sitting on the bench up there, he'd think she was one of those water-sprites he was always telling us about — come over from Scotland to visit him!'

'He might, at that,' Doyle laughed back, leaning out of the opening to watch as Aisling, jeans and T-shirt clinging to her slight figure and fair hair dripping over her shoulders, was lifted over the barrier. The next minute her head appeared again, and she was pointing down in their direction.

'Thank God,' Desmond said. He eased his bulky frame into as comfortable a position as he could in the cramped space, shut his eyes and relaxed slightly. Still, he couldn't disguise the fact that his legs were shaking. 'Now all we have to do is wait,' he told the others.

Doyle, crouching behind him, nodded. Behind him, Claire and Brendan were huddled against the pipe. Claire was hugging the targe to her chest, her eyes dreamy, staring across the river. Was she trying to imagine what it had been like a thousand years ago? wondered Doyle— picturing herself in one of the caves, looking over at the early-Viking settlement? Or was she thinking about how delighted her father would be when he learned about the targe and the axe-head? Would they be enough to warrant an archaeological dig and restore Professor Kiely's faith in himself? For Claire's sake, Doyle certainly hoped so. Claire caught his look and smiled, but said nothing.

She and Aisling weren't so very different in some ways, Doyle realised. Her need to know the truth about the long-past incident was driven by the bond between her and her father — just as Aisling's willing-ness to go along with the van driver's orders, and then her determination to have the men caught, were for her father's sake.

Could I ever be that close to my parents? wondered Doyle. Maybe not, but at least things at home are better now — and they'll probably get even better, he thought contentedly. He must remember to tell Brendan about the lighthouse trip his father had promised ....

He glanced at Brendan, who was sitting in silence. Maybe he was still smarting from Desmond's rebuke — not that Brendan was one to sulk or hold a grudge. His joke about the Semtex had been a bit close to the bone, but — Doyle grinned to himself at the thought — it had been pretty funny! And, to be fair, without Brendan's buoyant nature they might well have sunk into despair. Perhaps, though, Brendan — like himself — was thinking about Claire's and Aisling's relationships with their fathers, and wondering about his own father ....

Brendan looked up, as though sensing the stare. As his hand reached towards a pocket, Doyle remembered the other thing he had found.

'Brendan, what —' he began; then he stopped, as Brendan's eyes widened and his mouth fell open. At the same moment there was a startled gasp from Desmond.

In the mouth of the pipe, the face of a bearded man had appeared from nowhere. It was staring at Desmond, who had opened his eyes to find it only a few inches from his own face.

Claire dissolved in giggles verging on hysteria, as the face spoke. 'Right, you lot,' it said, 'let's get you out of there.'

Desmond recovered quickly. 'Take it easy, Claire,' he told her gently, as the figure of a man swung round in front of the opening.

'Brendan looked like he'd seen a ghost,' she said, swallowing hard and biting her lip.

'I thought I had!' Brendan declared. 'One of your Highlanders — except they didn't have Garda uniforms,' he added.

The guard was attached to a harness and held another in his hand. He lowered himself down until he was level with the lower edge of the opening.

'It's yourself, Desmond, is it?' he said. 'Who do you want out first?'

Desmond flushed slightly — whether from embarrass-ment or from pleasure at the guard's assumption that he should decide, Doyle wasn't sure. Certainly the guard looked on Desmond — as they all had — as the leader.

Desmond hesitated and then asked, 'Have the guards gone to Paddy's Cove?'

'Indeed they have,' the guard answered grimly. He looked beyond them, into the pipe. 'They'll not risk moving anything, though, until you're all out of there. So who's it to be?'

'Claire,' Desmond said, turning, 'can you get past Doyle?'

Doyle edged back, and Claire scrambled to the edge of the opening.

'You bringing that with you?' the guard asked, indicating the targe. 'Can't you leave it?'

'No way.'

'Right,' he told her. 'But you'll have to hang on to it.'

Steadying himself with his feet on the wall below, he swung the spare harness round. 'Desmond,' he said, 'can you put this on her?'

'You'll be fine,' Desmond reassured Claire, as he helped her slip into the harness. 'But give me your glasses, in case they fall off into the river.'

Claire looked down, and her face went white. 'I don't think I can ....' she whispered, as the guard put out a hand to pull her towards him.

'Of course you can.' The guard was brisk and business-like. 'Just don't look down.' He signalled to someone above, and swung Claire outwards. 'See,' he said, 'it's simple. Here we go.'

'You next, Doyle. Then Brendan,' Desmond said decisively. 'I'll follow.'

THIRTY

As the guards ushered Doyle and the others into a van, Doyle realised that the whole area had been cordoned off. The guards would give them no information; in answer to all their questions, they simply said, 'You'll hear about it all in good time.' With that they had to be content, although Brendan complained loudly as they tidied themselves in the washroom at the Garda station, only calming down when a young guard told them to go to the interview room.

Entering the room, Doyle looked around in surprise. In his mind had been the scene he had seen so often on television: a windowless room, bare except for two chairs and a table, austere and uninviting. This was a large, airy room, with comfortable chairs arranged in groups. Doyle suddenly realised that it was actually the station staff room.

Aisling was there already, sitting within the crook of her father's arm. She was wearing a new pair of designer jeans and a pretty T-shirt; someone must have gone across to a shop and bought her a change of clothing, Doyle realised.

'They've all been arrested!' she told the others gleefully. 'We were in time!'

'Thanks to you, Aisling,' Brendan told her. 'You were *magnificent*. Just brilliant!'

'She was, wasn't she?' Mr O'Leary said proudly, rising to shake hands with each of them. 'Weren't you all! I can't thank you enough. But here comes the Superintendent,' he added. 'He needs to have a word with you. I've given him a statement and Aisling has told her story. You'll need to fill in the blanks.'

The Superintendent smiled as he sat down. 'Make yourselves comfortable,' he told them.

Doyle glanced at Desmond, then down at his jeans. Their hands and faces were clean enough, but they could hardly sit on the chairs in their filthy clothes. Desmond pointed to his combat trousers and grimaced at the young guard.

'I'll get four chairs from the interview room,' he told them with a grin.

The Superintendent listened gravely to what they had to say, interrupting occasionally to ask a question. Only once did he show any disapproval at the way they had behaved.

'You knew, then, that the café dealt drugs?' he asked, looking at Desmond. 'You didn't mention it to your father? You are Frank Kiely's son, aren't you?'

Desmond flushed and looked at the floor. Doyle felt a wave of sympathy for him, but it was Brendan who butted in. 'It was only hash,' he said defensively.

'Unfortunately, money from the sale of the cannabis would have helped buy the Semtex,' the Superintendent pointed out. 'That's something you young ones don't realise: many sinister organisations are funded by drug sales. And cannabis *is* illegal,' he added mildly. 'But fair enough,' he went on, to Desmond. 'My own father was in the force. I haven't forgotten what it was like to be a guard's son! Yes?' he asked, as the door opened and a young woman looked in. 'What is it?'

'The men from Customs, sir,' she told him.

'Bring them in.'

Doyle flushed as his father entered the room. He knew that he, as much as Desmond, should have said something about the drugs.

'Everything in order?' the Superintendent asked.

Mr Whelan nodded. 'Yes. You'll have our report in the morning.'

'Fine. Thanks.' The Superintendent swept an arm around the room. 'Here are the youngsters who did our job for us.'

'Doyle!' Mr Whelan gave an exclamation of surprise and concern. 'Of course — I should have realised. You said you were going to the harbour. My son,' he explained to the Superintendent.

The Superintendent laughed. 'Well, at least we were well represented,' he said, indicating Desmond. 'You've met Detective Sergeant Kiely, I think. This is Desmond, his son.'

'And that's Brendan, I think.' Doyle's father smiled at them all. 'Who's Aisling and who's Claire?' he asked.

As Doyle introduced the girls, he marvelled that his father had actually remembered their names. It was more than he could have hoped for.

'Claire?' The Superintendent looked at her closely. 'Of course. I thought I recognised you. Claire Kiely, isn't it? I've seen you up at the National Library. My wife works there. She speaks highly of you. I've been wondering what it is you're holding on to so tightly,' he added.

'A targe.' Claire held it out for his inspection. 'We found it in the drain.' Her face fell suddenly. 'We won't have to leave it here, will we?' she asked desperately.

'No, I shouldn't think so.' The Superintendent smiled at her as he examined the targe. 'Not for the moment, anyway. It's very interesting, though — and it might help to vindicate your father's theory.'

'You read the article?' Claire asked breathlessly.

'Yes. I'm a member of a historical society, and we discussed it at the time. There were a good few of us who were disappointed about all the criticism that was made; we thought the theory should have been looked into. I wonder —'

Brendan interrupted. 'Janey,' he exclaimed, 'I nearly forgot!' He pulled something out of his pocket, spilling earth onto the carpeted floor.

His flustered apologies went unnoticed as Claire gave a shriek of pure delight. 'Brendan! Was that what you found?'

'Too right,' Brendan said, holding it out towards her as they all crowded round. 'Now everyone will know that your father's not ... that your father was right.'

Claire's hand was shaking so much she could hardly lift the coin. It was dirty, but the gold glint was unmistakable. She rubbed it gently and lovingly with a tissue pulled from her pocket, pushed at the legs of her spectacles, and then peered at it closely.

'It is!' she cried triumphantly. 'It's one of the newly minted coins Da said were there! Wait till I tell him!'

She would have handed it back to Brendan, but he shook his head. 'No,' he said, 'you keep it.'

'Maybe none of us can,' Desmond said doubtfully, with a glance at the Superintendent. 'Is it treasure trove, or something like that?'

'I don't think one coin counts,' the Superintendent told them. 'And if we find the others, I see no reason why you shouldn't each get one.' He looked at Claire. 'Take it to show your father,' he told her. 'Though I might borrow it, and the targe, later. And tell him to re-publish that article. He shouldn't have too much

trouble getting permission for a dig. That café will be
closed down anyway — and the hole in their yard will
have to be investigated. I don't think there will be
any problem. It's an amazing coincidence that these
discoveries should be made almost exactly one thousand
years after the event,' he added in an awed voice.
'Amazing.'

Not really all that much of a coincidence, Doyle
thought. But then, no one had told the Superintendent
about the project.

And what a start that was off to! They had the two
newly minted coins — a perfect base to build on ....

'I'll drop Claire and Desmond off,' Mr O'Leary was
saying. 'What about the others?'

'We had our bikes,' Doyle put in. 'They're up the
lane from Paddy's Cove.'

'I'll run you both over,' his father told him. 'Then
you can cycle home.' He looked at his watch. 'Your
mother should be home by then, I think.'

'Did you ask Brendan about the lighthouse visit?' Mr
Whelan asked as they drew up near the café, just outside the police cordon.

'What's that, then?' Brendan wanted to know.

'I didn't get round to it, with all the excitement,'
Doyle said. 'Dad's arranged to take us to look around
the fishing-harbour lighthouse,' he explained to Brendan,
'if you want to come.'

'Try and stop me.' Brendan grinned at them both.

Doyle's father laughed. 'Right,' he said, 'that's
settled. Next Sunday it is. Now get your bikes. Come
back with Doyle if you like, Brendan,' he added. 'Join
us for a meal.'

'Cool! I'd love that.'

Brendan beamed as Mr Whelan drove off. 'He's sound, Doyle,' he exclaimed. 'Imagine taking us to look round the lighthouse! Wait till I tell Mam! I'd better change into clean jeans before we head for your gaff, though — Gran will murder me if I say I'm going out in these clothes.' He grinned. 'Will you come in while I change? Gran's probably making pancakes .... Anyway, if I'm going shares in your da, you should have a share of my gran. Are you on?'

'Count me in,' Doyle told him.

Count me in. Magic words.

Up until the last few weeks, he had always been on the outside.

What a start to the new millennium!

Author's Note

The story of the Highlanders coming to Ireland to fight Brian Boru, and being buried in a cave with their treasure, is pure fiction. Only the background of the story — the time, the place, and the battle — is historical fact. I have also taken a few liberties with Dublin geography, for the sake of the story.